G
13



Gallery 13

New York London Toronto Sydney New Delhi

PIMITAMON
PIMITAMON
OPP
The PIT STOP
SKY RANCH DINER
BUD LITE
THAT'S HIM?
The PIT STOP

WHERE?
AT THE BAR OVER THERE.
SURE LOOKS LIKE HIM.
HUH.
WHAT?
THOUGHT HE'D BE *BIGGER.*
...DON'T *LOOK* SO TOUGH.

HEY, DEREK, BUY ME A DRINK?
NOT TONIGHT, LISA. NOT FEELING SO HOT.
OH, POOR BABY. MAYBE I CAN MAKE YOU FEEL BETTER?
NOT TONIGHT, LISA.
OH, COME ON, DEREK. WE HAVEN'T HUNG OUT ALL WEEK. I MISS YOU.
I SAID, *NOT TONIGHT.*
MEN
FTTT!
ASSHOLE.
MEN
GERRY, TURN THE GAME UP. HABS ARE ON.

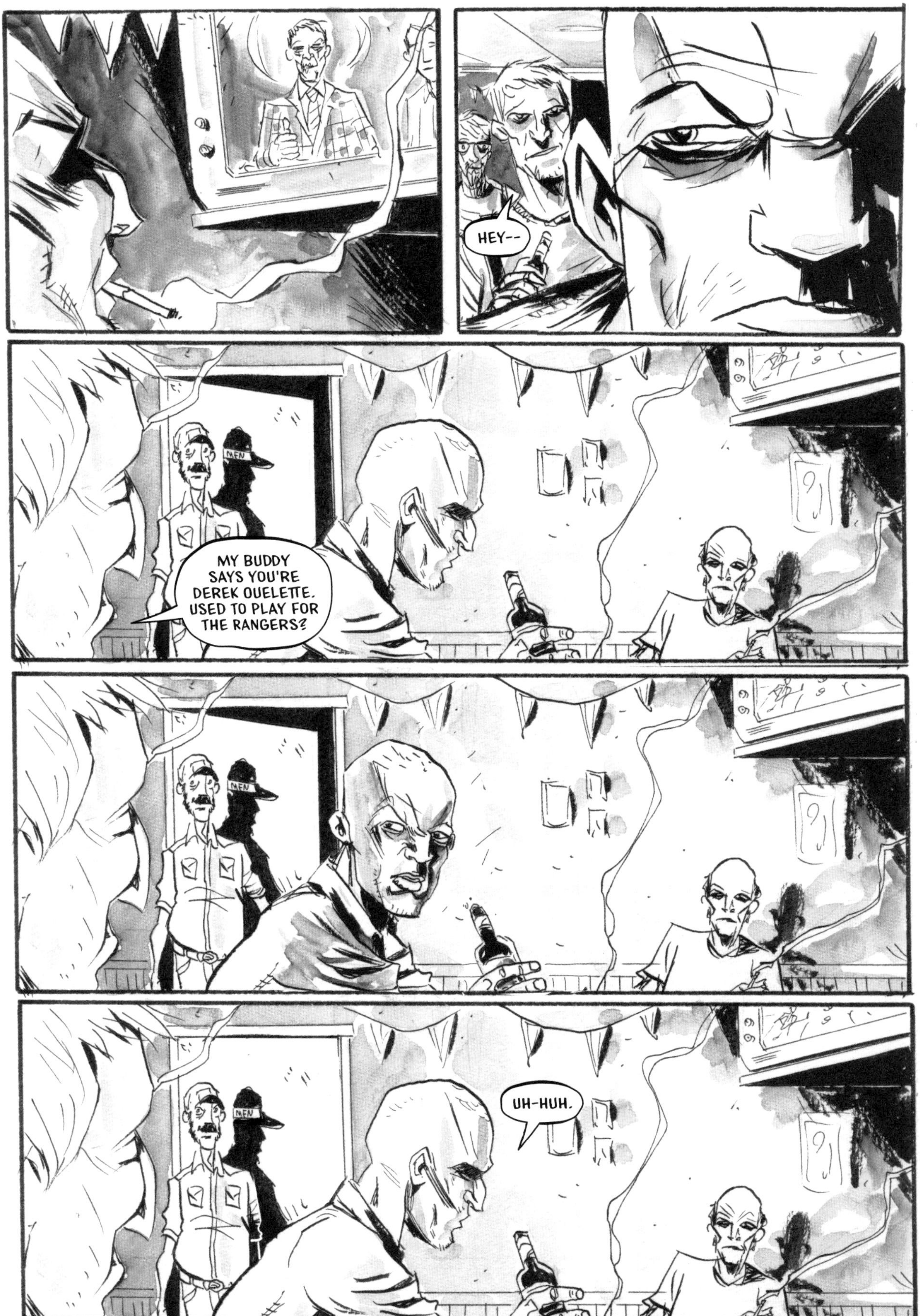
HEY--
MY BUDDY SAYS YOU'RE DEREK OUELETTE. USED TO PLAY FOR THE RANGERS?
UH-HUH.

REMY PAPINEAU. ME AND MY BUDDY ARE JUST UP SNOWMOBILING NEAR THE MOOSE RIVER.
WE'RE BIG FANS OF YOURS.
WHAT? YOU TOO GOOD TO SHAKE OUR HANDS?
BIG MAN, USED TO PLAY IN THE NHL, TOO GOOD FOR US, EH?
COME ON, REMY...
JUST TRYIN' TO WATCH THE GAME, BUD.
KNOW WHAT I THINK?
THINK YOU'RE JUST SOME CEMENT HEAD WHO TOOK ONE TOO MANY PUNCHES. THINK *YOU* AIN'T SO TOUGH AS YOU THINK...*BUD.*

THUNK!

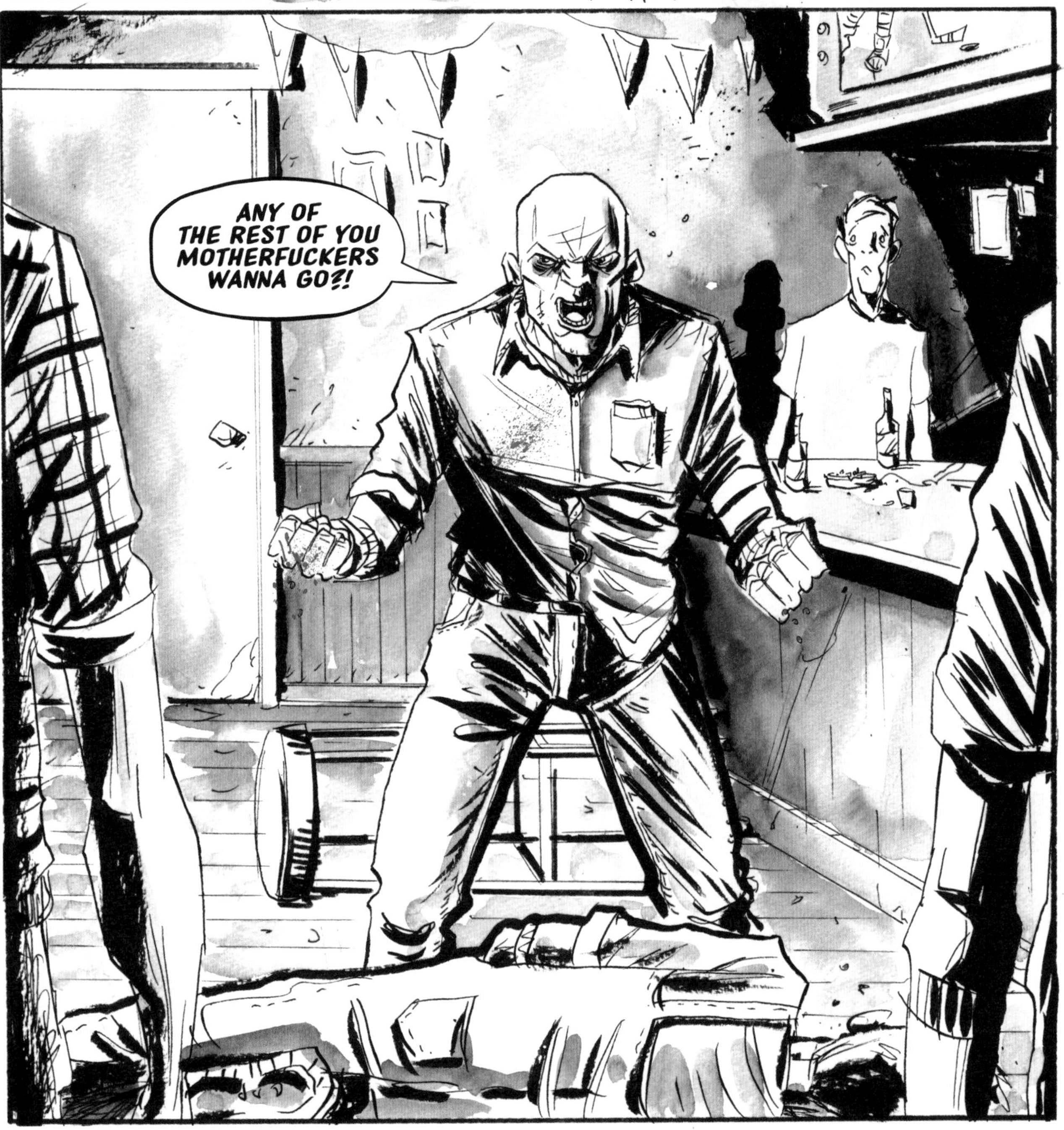
ANY OF THE REST OF YOU MOTHERFUCKERS WANNA GO?!

ROUGH

INECK

PANT-PANT-PANT
PANT-PANT-PANT..
WHAT ARE YOU LOOKING AT?
ARK!
O.P.P.
ZIP!

CHRIST, DEREK, COULDN'T YOU AT LEAST GO **BEHIND** THE BUILDING? SOME KID COULD SEE YOU OR SOMETHING.
DON'T SEE NO KIDS AROUND.
NOT REALLY THE POINT.
YOU KNOW I GOTTA TAKE YOU TO THE STATION NOW, RIGHT?
FOR WHAT, RAY? PISSING AGAINST A WALL?
NO, SMART-ASS, FOR BEATING THAT SNOWMOBILER WITHIN AN INCH OF HIS DAMN LIFE.
GUY ASKED FOR IT.
NOT REALLY THE POINT.

YOU GOT A BOTTLE IN HERE, OR WHAT? I DIDN'T GET A CHANCE TO PICK UP MY PRESCRIPTION TODAY.
HAVEN'T YOU HAD ENOUGH TONIGHT?
AND I'M SERIOUS. I GOTTA TAKE YOU IN.
NO YOU DON'T. WE PLAYED FUCKING PEEWEE TOGETHER, RAY. DON'T *GOTTA* DO NOTHING.
NOW, I KNOW YOU GOT A MICKEY IN HERE SOMEWHERE.
JESUS.
WHERE'S YOUR COAT? AREN'T YOU FREEZING?
FORGOT IT IN THE BAR.
JESUS.
QUIT SAYING THAT. YOU'RE PISSING ME OFF.

OH YEAH? WHAT ARE YOU GONNA DO? BEAT THE FUCK OUT OF ME, TOO? I'M PRETTY MUCH THE LAST GUY IN *THE PIT* YOU AIN'T BEAT UP YET.
WAIT... *YOU'RE* A GUY?
HAHA. GOOD ONE. ASSHOLE.
HOW ARE YOUR HEADACHES, ANYWAY? STILL SEEING THAT DOCTOR DOWN IN COCHRANE?
NAH...DON'T DO ANY GOOD ANYWAY.
HOW YOU SUPPOSED TO KNOW IF YOU DON'T KEEP GOING?

...'NIGHT, RAY.
WHATTA YOU MEAN, GOOD NIGHT? I REALLY GOTTA TAKE YOU IN, DEREK.
HEY! YOU CAN'T JUST WALK AWAY!
...WHAT ABOUT MY BOTTLE!?
OPP

Pimitamon
ARENA
..CRUNCH—CRUNCH..CRUNCH..
HOME 00

JANITORIAL
JANITORIAL
SHIT.

CRUNCH..
CRUNCH..CRUNCH..
..CRUNCH..
FUCK.

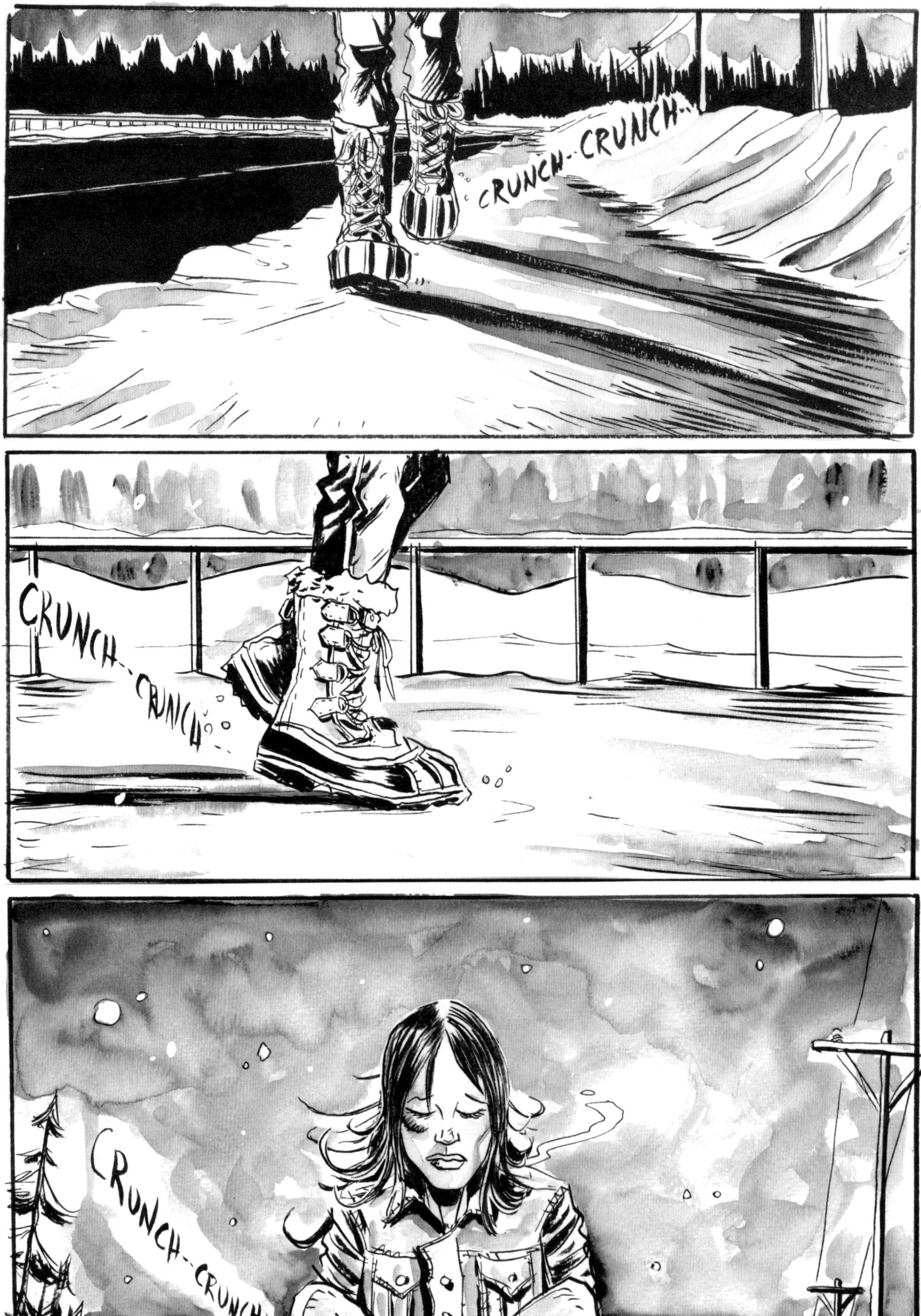
CRUNCH--CRUNCH--
CRUNCH--
CRUNCH--CRUNCH
CRUNCH--CRUNCH

MOTEL
CRUNCH
CRUNCH

OPEN 24 hrs
HUSKY
RESTAURANT
OPEN 24 HOURS
CRUNCH..
CRUNCH..
CRUNCH

RESTAURANT
OPEN
CRUNCH - CRUNCH
HEY, WHERE YOU GOING, SWEETHEART?
FUCK OFF.
GOT A MOUTH ON HER.
DING!
I'LL SAY.

HELP YOU?
...COFFEE?
JESUS, GIRL. YOU'RE FREEZING! WHAT YOU DOING OUT THERE DRESSED LIKE THAT?
I--
I WAS IN A BIT OF A RUSH.
OH!

WELL...LET ME GET THAT COFFEE.
THANKS.
SO, UH... YOU STAYIN' UP AT THE **PINE LODGE?**
YEAH. I MEAN, I WAS, ANYWAY.
WITH YOUR...WHAT, BOYFRIEND? TOO YOUNG TO BE MARRIED, I HOPE?
BOYFRIEND. EX. I'M LEAVING.
...GOOD FOR YOU. WHERE YOU HEADED?
UP NORTH. PIMITAMON.
GOT SOME FAMILY UP THERE.
THE PIT? THAT'S A LONG WAYS. YOU GOT ANY MONEY, HON?

NO.
WELL, I WOULDN'T BE HITCHING A RIDE WITH THE LIKES OF THEM IF I WAS YOU. END UP BACK IN THE SAME MESS YOU ARE NOW.
YEAH. I KNOW.
LOOK. I GOT A COUPLE ROOMS OUT BACK. IT AIN'T MUCH, BUT YOU CAN HAVE ONE FOR A NIGHT OR TWO IF YOU WANT.
THANKS, BUT...I SHOULD BE GOING.
YOU SURE YOU DON'T WANT TO STAY THE NIGHT, HON?
YEAH. I'M SURE.

WELL... DON'T WORRY ABOUT THE COFFEE.
OH. THANKS.
HOLD ON A SECOND.
I SHOULDN'T BE DOING THIS, BUT THERE'S A BUS COMES THROUGH HERE AROUND ELEVEN HEADING NORTH. WHY DON'T YOU WAIT HERE AND TAKE THAT.
YOU SURE?
I'M SURE.
THANKS.

LEAST I CAN DO. NOW SIT DOWN AND FINISH YOUR COFFEE.
TOO DAMN COLD TO WAIT OUTSIDE.
DING!
HUMPH!

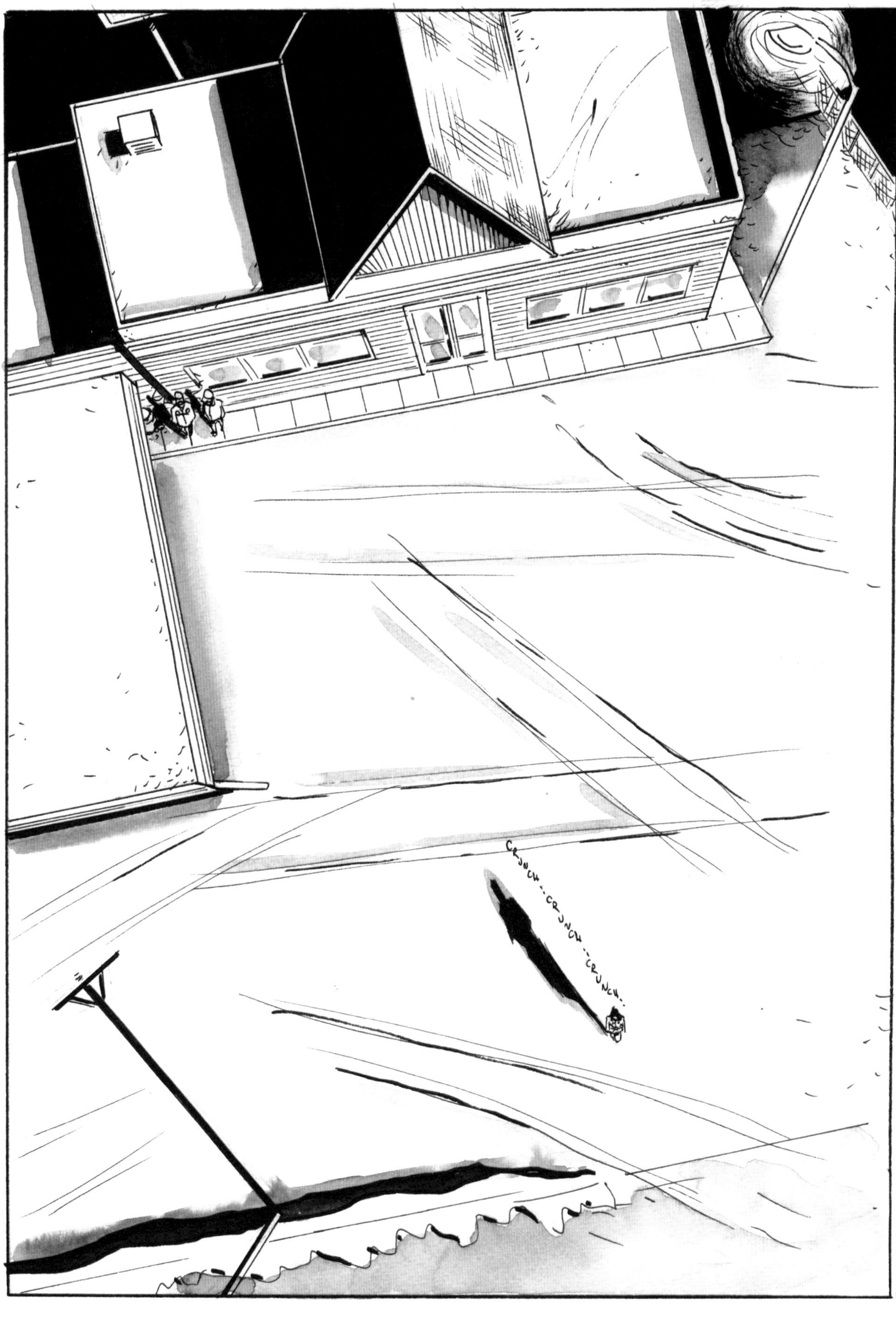
CRUNCH..CRUNCH..CRUNCH..

PIMITAMON
Pimitamon
ARENA

DEREK?
DEREK, WAKE UP!
--HRRN...?

--THE FUCK?
YOU TELL ME, TOUGH GUY. THE HELL YOU DOING OUT HERE?
LEFT MY COAT AT THE BAR. KEYS WERE IN IT.

*SIGH*--WELL, COME ON, THEN. CAN'T STAY OUT HERE. BANTAMS GOT PRACTICE AT SEVEN.

GONNA HAVE TO HIDE A SPARE KEY FOR YOU SOMEWHERE, THIS KEEPS HAPPENING.
SORRY, AL.
UH-HUH...
JAN
YOU GOT WORK THIS MORNING?
WHAT DAY IS IT?
SATURDAY, GENIUS.
FLIK!
FUCK.
YEAH. I GOTTA GET GOING SOON.
WELL...DON'T FORGET YOUR KEYS THIS TIME.
JANITOR

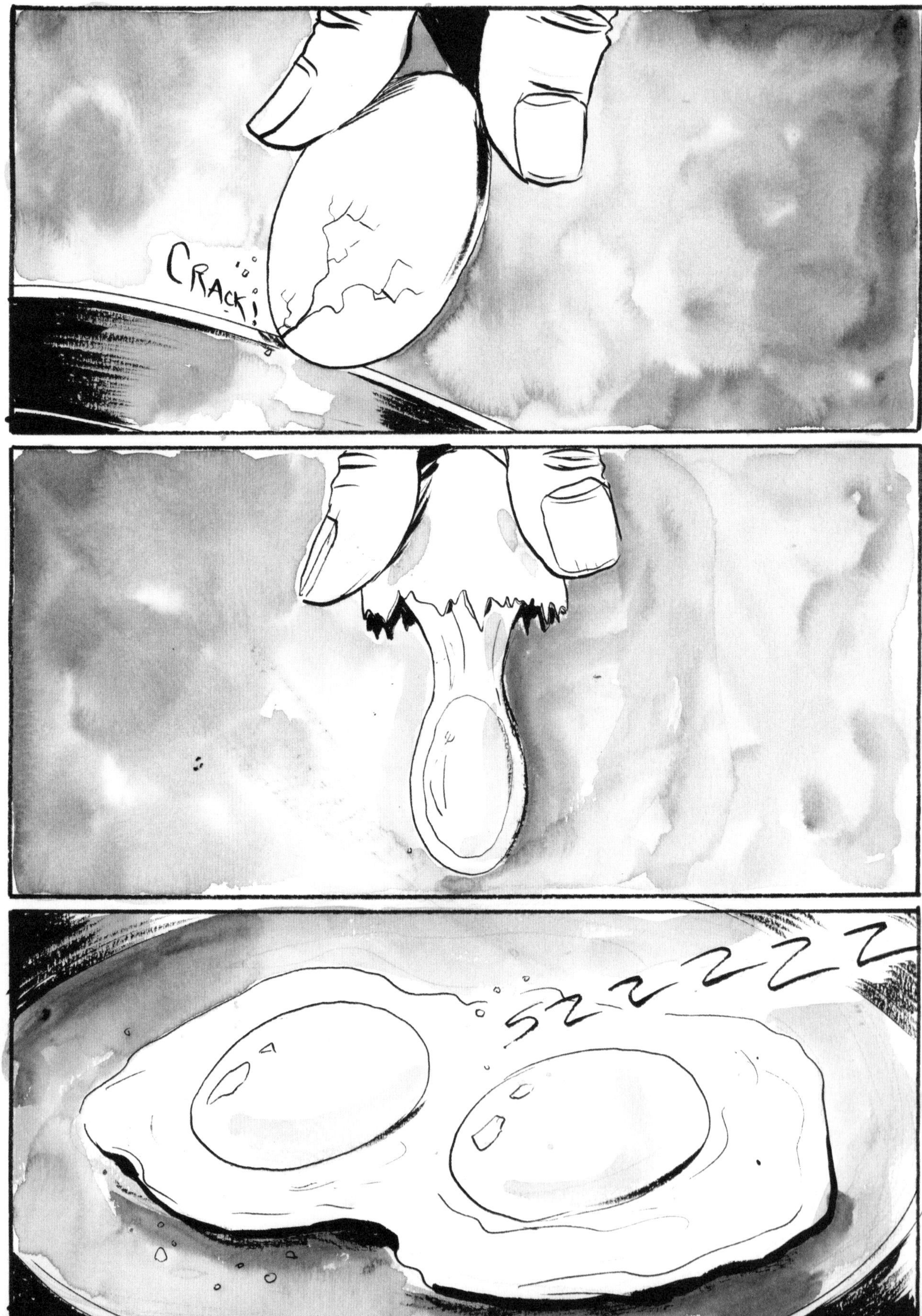
CRACK!
SZZZZZZ

SZZZZZZ

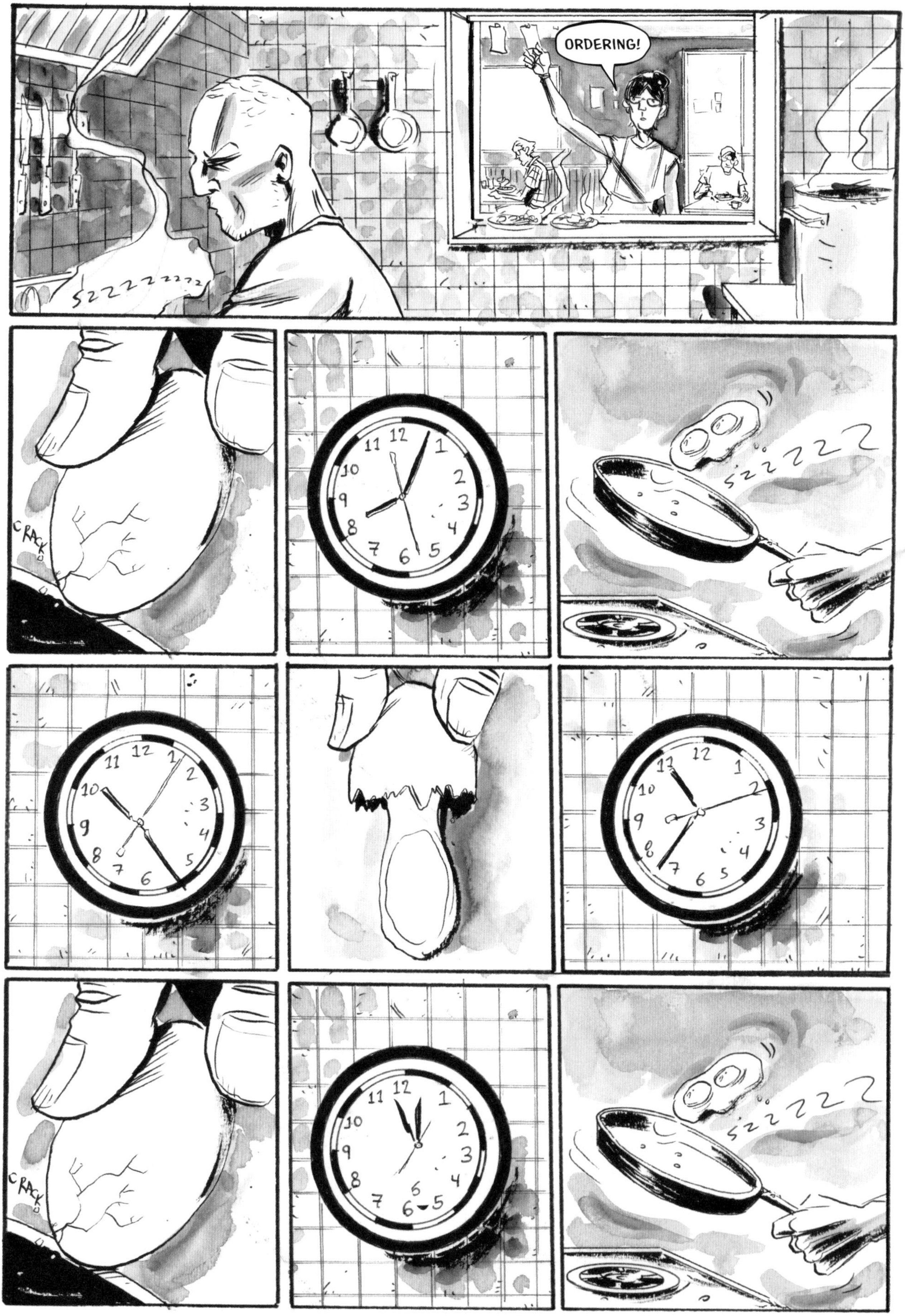
ORDERING!
SZZZZZZZZ
CRACK
SZZZZZZ
CRACK
SZZZZZZ

FTTT!

LOCK
DOOR!

--PANT-- PANT--
PANT--PANT--

SLAM

CRUNCH-CRUNCH..
TIMMINS
TIMMINS THUNDERCATS
CRUNCH..CRUNCH..
AL.
HEY, TOUGH GUY.

WE'RE UP ONE NOTHING, FIRST PERIOD.
THESE TIMMINS GUYS ANY GOOD?
EXIT
PRETTY SHIT, EXCEPT FOR THAT DEFENSEMAN.
WHICH ONE?
"NUMBER EIGHTEEN. BIG KID.
"HELL OF A SCRAPPER. AND HE'S GOT HANDS TOO.
"REMINDS ME OF YOU."

YOU EVER MISS IT?
I WAS NEVER REALLY A HOCKEY PLAYER, AL. I WAS JUST A THUG.
EXIT
AT LEAST NOW I DON'T HAVE TO PRETEND TO BE SOMETHING I'M NOT.
WHERE YOU GOING? YOU JUST GOT HOME.
OUT. IT'S TOO NOISY HERE.

SKI-DOO
EXIT
GIMME A BEER AND A SHOT, GERRY. AND TURN THE GAME UP.

YOU REALLY THINK I'M GOING TO SERVE YOU AFTER THAT SHIT YOU PULLED LAST NIGHT?
WHAT? YOU KIDDING, ME?
NO. FORGET IT, DEREK.
...FUCKING BULLSHIT.

LCBO
CRUNCH
CRUNCH CRUNCH!
10 WINES
HEY, KILLER.
DING!
DR. DAVE. NEED TO PICK UP MY PRESCRIPTION.
THOUGHT YOU'D BE AT THE BAR WATCHING THE GAME TONIGHT.
STAYING AWAY FROM THE BAR FOR A BIT.
YEAH...I HEARD YOU DROPPED THE GLOVES LAST NIGHT.
DING
GUY HAD IT COMING.
DON'T THEY ALL.

PIMITAMON

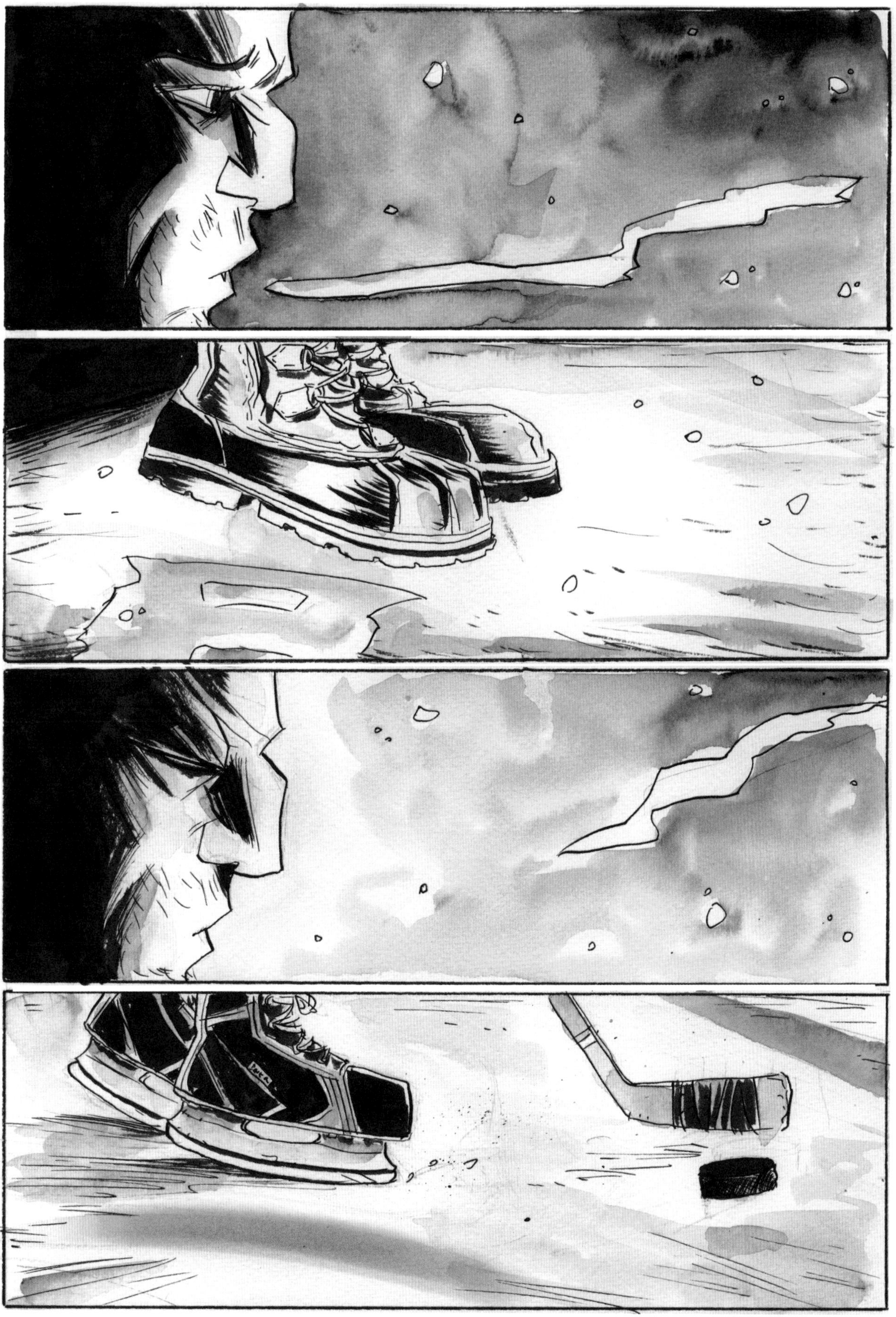

93
95
98

--UNGH!
THAT'S OKAY. SHAKE IT OFF, DEREK!

WHY'D YOU COME OFF?
I SAID, WHY'D YOU COME OFF THE ICE, DEREK?
DON'T KNOW.
YOU *DON'T KNOW?*

COME ON, PAT. I TOLD YOU, YOU CAN'T JUST COME BEHIND THE BENCH LIKE THIS.
I'M TALKING TO MY KID, TERRY. YOU GOT A PROBLEM WITH THAT?
SO, YOU GONNA LET THAT KID PUSH YOU AROUND LIKE THAT, OR WHAT?!
NO.

WHAT?
NO!
THEN MAN UP AND GET BACK OUT THERE!

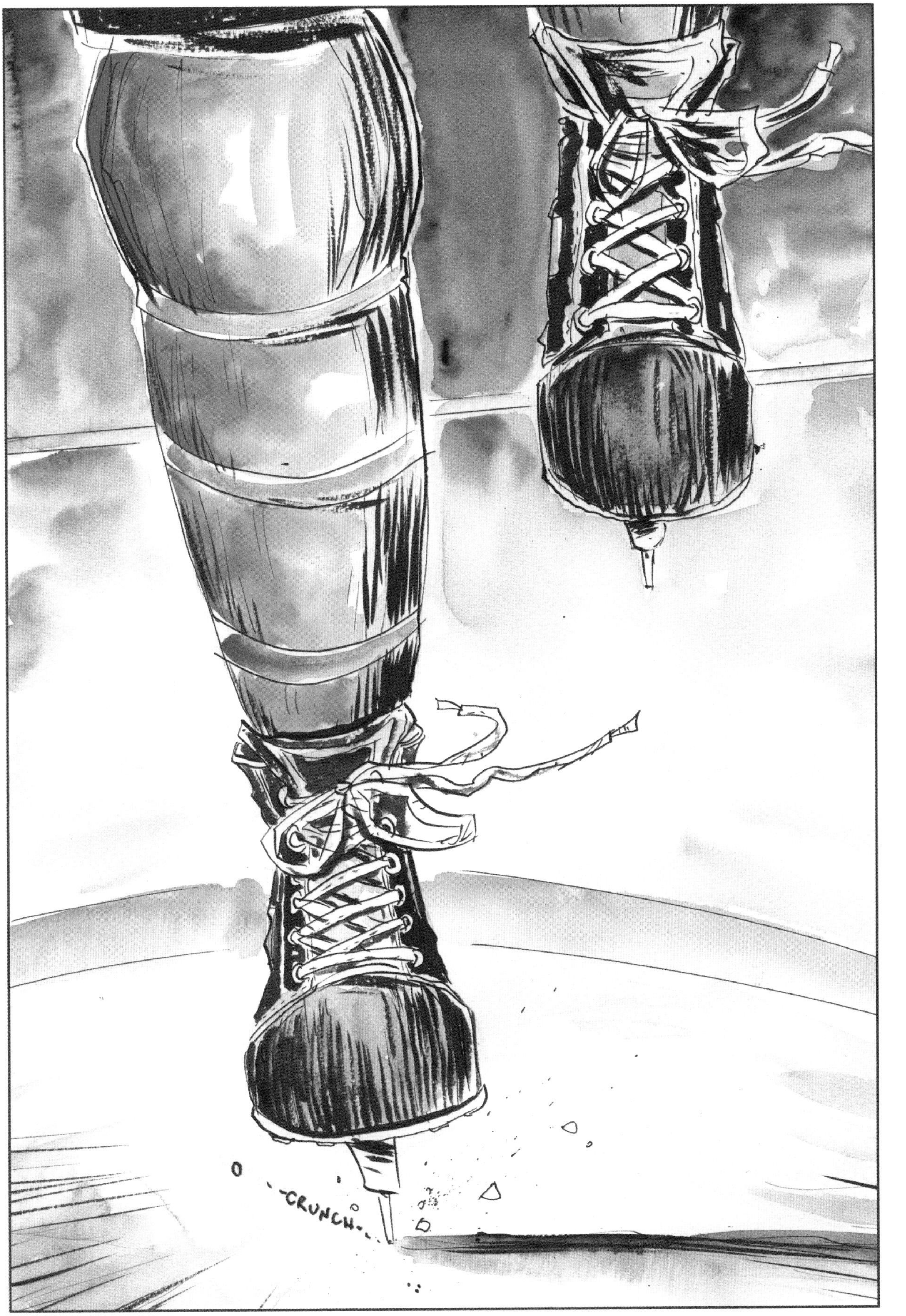
CRUNCH

CRUNCH
CRUNCH
CRUNCH
CRU

CH..
CRUN

THE HELL YOU DOING, DEREK?!

CRUNCH-- CRUNCH-
HEY, UH...YOU'RE DEREK OUELETTE, RIGHT?
MINS
TIMMINS
YEAH.
CRUNCH--CRUNCH--
HOLY SHIT! WE LITERALLY WATCHED ALL OF YOUR FIGHTS ON YOUTUBE LAST WEEK!
YEAH, MAN, WE ARE SUCH HUGE FANS!
THAT FIGHT WITH BOUCHER WAS SICK!
YEAH... THANKS.

HEY, MAN, CAN WE GET A PICTURE WITH YOU?
--I DON'T THINK SO.
COME ON, MAN! JUST ONE? PLEASE. OUR BUDDIES WILL NEVER BELIEVE THIS.
...OKAY. JUST A QUICK ONE.
SWEET!
CHK!

SICK!
SO, HOW COME YOU'RE NOT PLAYING ANYMORE?
DUDE. DON'T YOU KNOW? HE CHOPPED SOME GUY RIGHT ACROSS THE FACE! LIKE A FUCKING TOMAHAWK, RIGHT?
LOOK, IT WAS NICE MEETING YOU GUYS, BUT I GOTTA GET TO BED.
WHAT... YOU LIVE HERE? AT THE RINK?
YOU'RE FUCKING WITH US, RIGHT?
YEAH. RIGHT. LATER, GUYS.

HEY, WAIT! CAN WE GET ONE MORE PICTURE FIRST?
...I DON'T THINK SO.
AW, COME ON, MAN! JUST ONE MORE.
I SAID NO.
FINE. JESUS. YOU DON'T HAVE TO BE A DICK ABOUT IT.

WHAT THE FUCK HAPPENED TO YOU, MAN?
FUCKING HAS-BEEN.

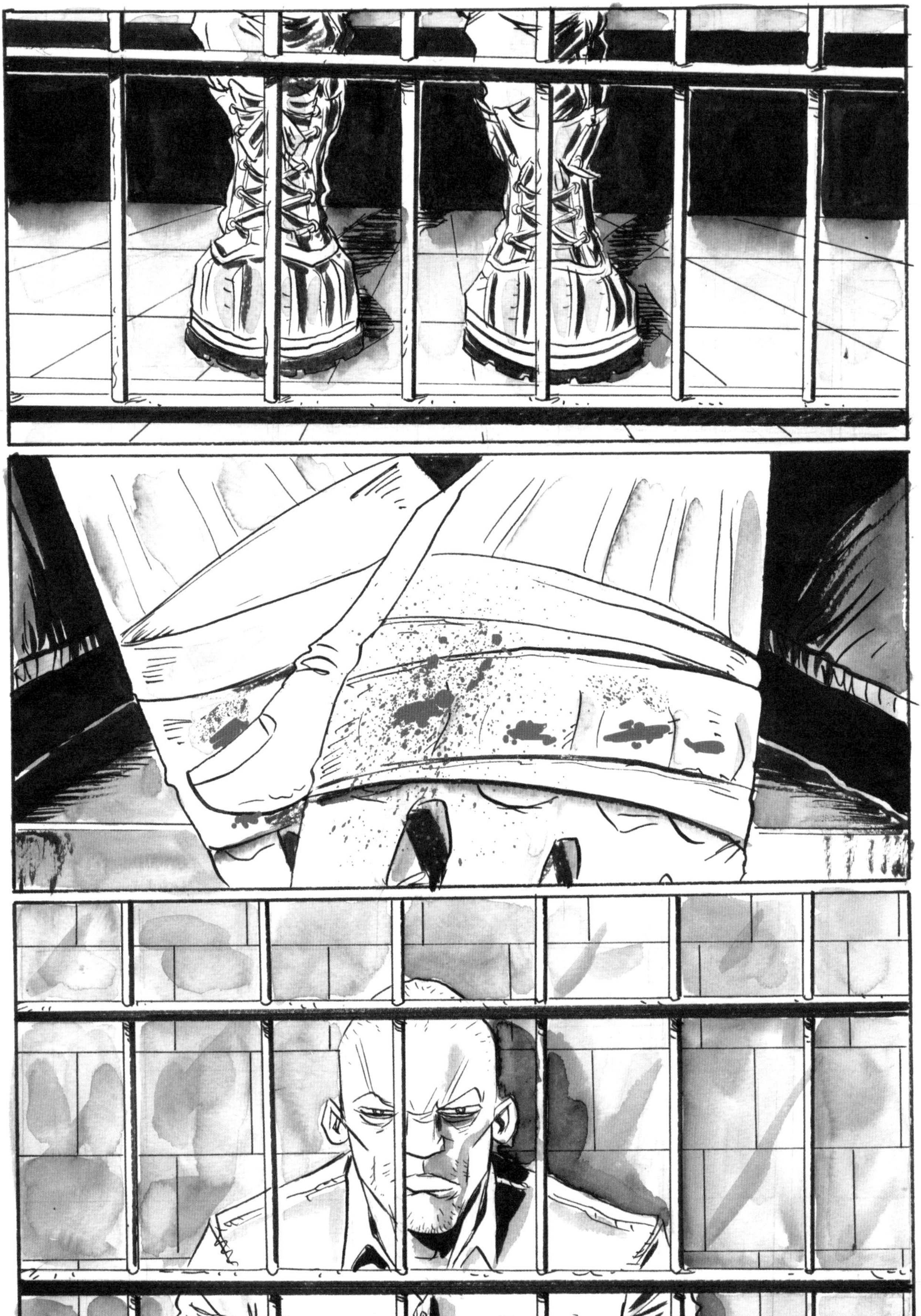

DEREK?

...SO I JUST GOT FINISHED TALKING TO THE KIDS.
I THINK THAT ONE KID IS ACTUALLY PROUD OF THE BROKEN NOSE YOU GAVE HIM.
WHAT THE HELL WERE YOU THINKING, DEREK?
I WASN'T.
NO SHIT. YOU GOT LUCKY TONIGHT. IF THAT KID DECIDED TO PRESS CHARGES, YOU'D BE FUCKED WITH YOUR RECORD.
I JUST--I DON'T KNOW WHAT TO SAY ANYMORE. I'M SICK OF LECTURING YOU ABOUT THIS SHIT.
YOU GOTTA STOP THIS, DEREK. YOU HAVE TO.

WELL? AREN'T YOU GOING TO SAY ANYTHING?
CAN I GO?
...
YEAH. I GUESS SO.
THANKS.

FUCK!
·sigh··

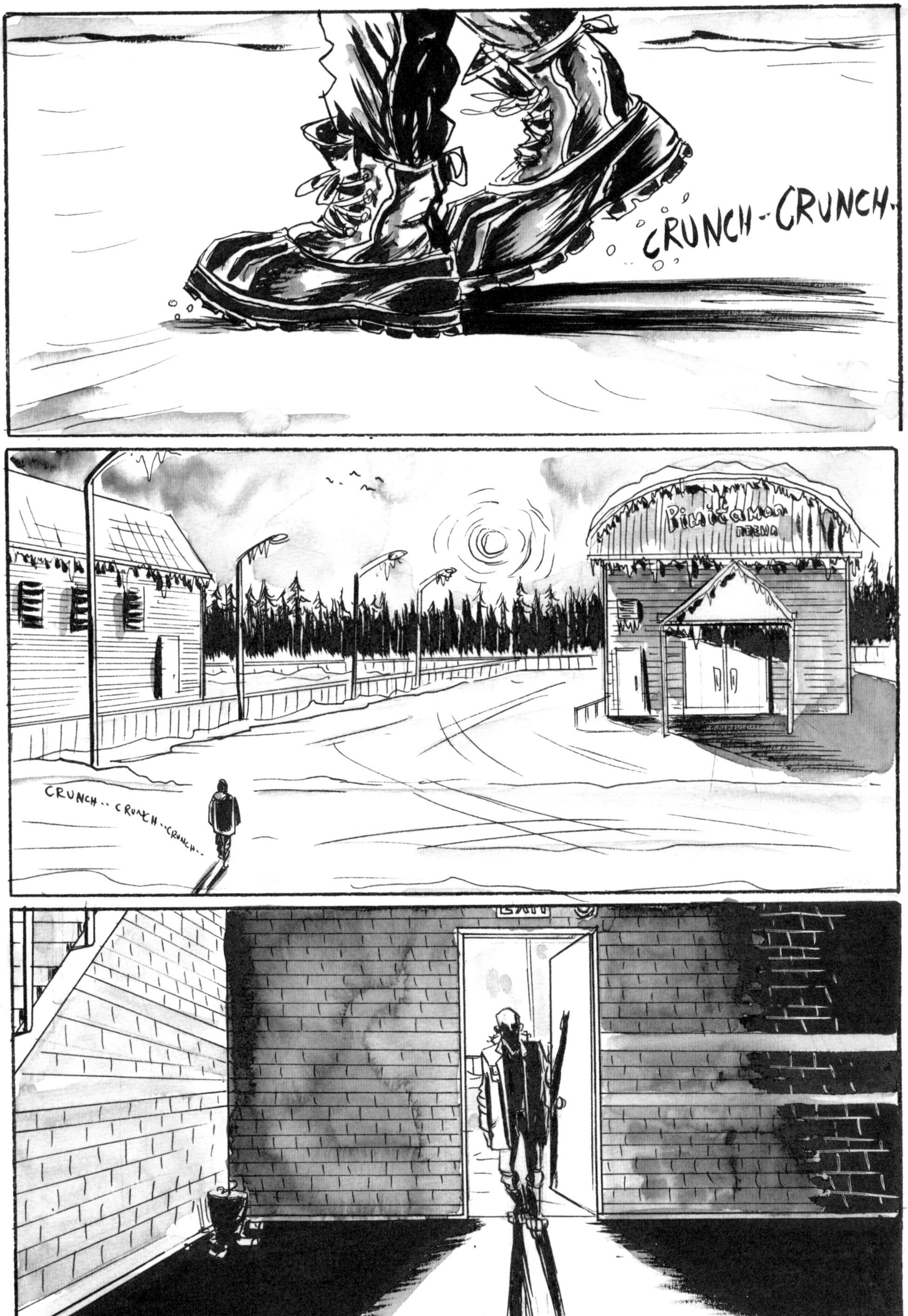
CRUNCH--CRUNCH--
Pimitamon
ARENA
CRUNCH.. CRUNCH..CRUNCH..

JANITORIAL
HEY, BIG BROTHER...
...LONG TIME NO SEE.

CRUNCH-CRUNCH-.
CRUNCH--CRUNCH-.

WI-FI
TV
BREAKFAST
SPECIAL
$4.99
CLOSED

--SORRY, I GOTTA PREP THE KITCHEN. YOU CAN SIT OUT HERE. I'LL PUT ON SOME COFFEE.
S'OKAY. I'LL COME WITH YOU.
GOD...THIS PLACE LOOKS EXACTLY THE SAME AS WHEN MOM WORKED HERE.
YEAH.
IT'S THE PIT. NOTHING CHANGES.
YEAH.
YOU OKAY? YOU SEEM...
JUST TIRED. WHAT ARE THOSE?

TYLENOL. GOT A HEADACHE. WANT ONE?
NO.
SO...WHAT ARE YOU DOING BACK, BETH?
I--
JEANIE MCKOGEE SAID SHE THOUGHT YOU WERE IN TORONTO.
SUN VALLEY
POTATOES
I WAS. FOR A WHILE.
CHOP!
...
I WENT LOOKING FOR YOU ONCE, YOU KNOW?

WHAT?! WHEN?
YEARS AGO WHEN I WAS PLAYING FOR SUDBURY AND WE HAD A GAME IN TORONTO. I WENT WALKING DOWNTOWN. IT'S SO BIG THERE. I HAD NO IDEA WHERE TO START.
SMOKE?
YEAH.

SO...WHO GAVE YOU THAT BLACK EYE?
WHY? SO YOU CAN GO KICK HIS ASS FOR ME?
SOMETHING LIKE THAT. YEAH.
HIS NAME IS WADE.
WADE. AND *WHERE* IS WADE NOW?
DOWN SOUTH. TIMMINS.

I STILL DON'T GET IT. WHY'D YOU LEAVE? WHY'D YOU RUN AWAY?
ARE YOU FUCKING ***SERIOUS,*** DEREK? YOU LEFT ME HERE.
IT WASN'T THAT BAD.
OH, THAT'S EASY FOR YOU TO SAY!
YOU WERE OFF PLAYING HOCKEY ALL THE TIME, AND THEN YOU LEFT FOR SUDBURY.
YOU LEFT ME. I WAS ***THIRTEEN*** AND YOU LEFT ME ALONE HERE, DEREK!
WHAT THE HELL WAS I SUPPOSED TO DO? BRING YOU ALONG ON THE TEAM BUS?!

...I DON'T KNOW. I WAS ALONE HERE AND I HAD TO GET AWAY. THERE WAS...THERE WAS TOO MUCH BULLSHIT HERE.
SO, WHAT HAPPENED TO YOU? WHAT DID YOU DO?
TOOK THE BUS TO BARRIE. HITCHHIKED TO TORONTO.
I LIVED IN SHELTERS AND ON THE STREETS FOR THE FIRST COUPLE OF YEARS.
JESUS, BETHY.
WASN'T SO BAD...

AT FIRST IT JUST FELT GOOD TO GET AWAY FROM THE PIT. FELT FREE.
AND THE CITY WAS... IT WAS BIG AND SCARY, BUT ALSO EXCITING. AT FIRST...

MET SOME OTHER KIDS FROM AROUND HERE. NATIVE KIDS.
WE LOOKED OUT FOR ONE ANOTHER MOSTLY.
SUMMER WAS FINE. LIKE CAMPING OUT. WINTERS, NOT SO MUCH...

I CLEANED UP ABOUT FOUR YEARS AGO. GOT A JOB AS A WAITRESS DOWNTOWN.
...THEN I MET WADE. HE USED TO COME INTO THIS BAR I WORKED AT.
HE WAS GREAT AT FIRST.
THEN...
JESUS-- I'LL FUCKING KILL HIM.
DOESN'T MATTER NOW. I'M HERE AND HE'S NOT.

I GOTTA OPEN UP SOON.
OKAY... GUESS I'LL CRASH AT YOUR PLACE. I'M EXHAUSTED.
HEY...DO YOU HAVE A FEW BUCKS? I JUST WANT TO GRAB A FEW THINGS AND GET CLEANED UP A BIT.
UH, YEAH... SURE.
TWENTY OKAY? IT'S ALL I GOT.
YEAH. THANKS.

HEY, BETHY...
YEAH?
...
NOTHING. I'LL SEE YOU LATER, OK?
YEAH... LATER.

SKYRANCH DINER
The Pit Stop
---CRUNCH--CRUNCH--

HEY THERE, TOUGH GUY. WHAT'S SHAKING?
AL.
YOU SEEN BETHY YET?
BETH?!
**BETH IS HERE?!** YOU GOTTA BE SHITTING ME!
SHE SHOWED UP LAST NIGHT. COME ON. SHE'D LOVE TO SEE YOU.
WELL, HOLY SHIT!

GEEZ. CAN'T REMEMBER THE LAST TIME I SAW HER.
JANITORIAL
MAYBE SHE'S STILL ASLEEP. YOU GOT YOUR KEY?
YEAH. BUT SHOULDN'T WE JUST LET HER REST?
NAH. SHE'S BEEN IN HERE ALL--!
JANITORIAL

BETH!
BETHY! WAKE UP!

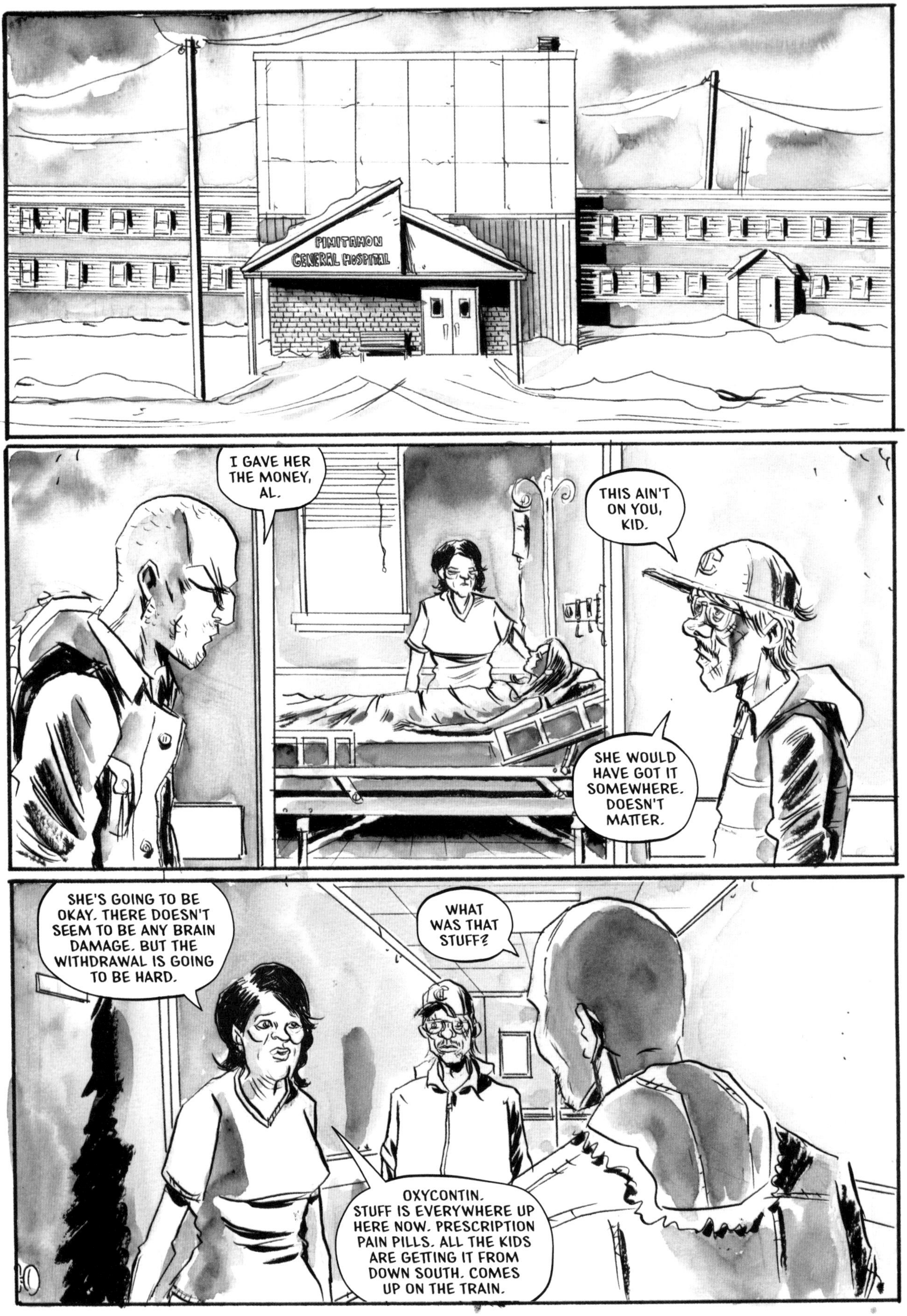
PIMITAMON GENERAL HOSPITAL
I GAVE HER THE MONEY, AL.
THIS AIN'T ON YOU, KID.
SHE WOULD HAVE GOT IT SOMEWHERE. DOESN'T MATTER.
SHE'S GOING TO BE OKAY. THERE DOESN'T SEEM TO BE ANY BRAIN DAMAGE. BUT THE WITHDRAWAL IS GOING TO BE HARD.
WHAT WAS THAT STUFF?
OXYCONTIN. STUFF IS EVERYWHERE UP HERE NOW. PRESCRIPTION PAIN PILLS. ALL THE KIDS ARE GETTING IT FROM DOWN SOUTH. COMES UP ON THE TRAIN.

JESUS!
THEY HAVE A DETOX DOWN IN TIMMINS. AS SOON AS SHE'S BETTER, WE SHOULD MOVE HER DOWN THERE. SHE NEEDS MORE HELP THAN WE CAN GIVE HER UP HERE.
AL, CAN YOU STAY HERE WITH HER A BIT?
WHY? WHERE THE HELL YOU GOING?!
DEREK?
DEREK?!

CRUNCH..
PIMITAN
CRUNCH... CRUNCH.. CRUNCH..
CRUNCH
CRUN

WHAT'S UP?
WHAT YOU NEED, MAN?

MOTHERFUCKERS!
HEY! WAIT!
NNNGG--

THAT WAS MY SISTER, YOU PIECE OF SHIT!

WHUP!
POLICE
POLICE
POLICE
ENOUGH!
STOP IT! DEREK! STOP!

WHAT THE FUCK WERE YOU THINKING?!
WHAT, YOU THINK YOU'RE *FUCKING BATMAN* NOW OR SOMETHING? HAVE YOU LOST YOUR *GODDAMN MIND*, DEREK!?
POLICE
IT'S BETH.
WHAT DID YOU SAY?
BETHY. SHE'S BACK.
O.P.P.
SCREEEECH

WHAT ARE YOU TALKING ABOUT?
YOU HEARD ME. BETH IS HOME. THOSE FUCKERS SOLD HER SOME OF THAT OXY SHIT. AL AND I FOUND HER IN MY ROOM.
IS SHE--
SHE'S AT THE HOSPITAL. AL'S WITH HER.
WAIT, HOW DO YOU KNOW IT WAS THOSE GUYS WHO SOLD TO HER?
DON'T BULLSHIT ME, RAY. YOU KNOW AS WELL AS I DO THOSE FUCKERS ARE THE ONES WHO DEAL THAT SHIT AROUND HERE. *YOU* SHOULD'VE ARRESTED THOSE FUCKS A LONG TIME AGO!

THIS IS NOT MY FAULT, DEREK!
FUCK. I KNOW THAT. I JUST--LOOK, YOU NEED TO TAKE ME BACK TO THE HOSPITAL.
ARE YOU INSANE!? DEREK, THERE IS NO WAY I CAN DO THAT. I'VE ALREADY CALLED THIS IN.
...THIS IS BETHY WE'RE TALKING ABOUT.

SQUEAK--SQUEAK...
WHERE THE HELL YOU BEEN?! SHE'S BEEN ASKING FOR YOU! TRIED TO WALK OUT OF HERE THREE TIMES. PRACTICALLY HAD TO TIE HER TO THE BED!
POLICE
RAY?
YEAH, IT'S ME, BETHY. YOU HAD US WORRIED SICK.
POLICE
I'M FINE. THIS IS ALL--I JUST NEED TO GET OUT OF HERE.
LIKE HELL YOU DO. WHAT THE HELL WERE YOU THINKING?!
EASY, DEREK.

RAY?
HEY, BRENDA. HOW IS SHE DOING?
SHE'LL LIVE, BUT NOT IF SHE KEEPS ON LIKE SHE IS. SHE NEEDS TO GET CLEANED UP, AND SHE'S NOT GOING TO BE ABLE TO DO IT ON HER OWN.
LIKE I SAID, THEY HAVE A REAL GOOD PROGRAM DOWN IN TIMMINS. WE COULD RELEASE HER DOWN THERE--
NO! NO WAY! I AM NOT DOING ANY *REHAB SHIT!* THIS IS GETTING BLOWN OUT OF PROPORTION!
MAYBE SHE'S RIGHT.
DON'T FUCKING ACT LIKE YOU KNOW ANYTHING ABOUT ME! YOU HAVEN'T SEEN ME SINCE I WAS THIRTEEN!
I--I CAN'T GO BACK TO TIMMINS, DEREK.

ARE YOU HANDLING THIS, RAYMOND? I'M OFF SHIFT SOON--
YEAH...I GOT IT, BRENDA. THANKS.
JESUS, BETH!
NO, BETH, I DIDN'T *RUN AND GET RAY!* CHRIST.
DON'T LOOK AT ME LIKE THAT! DID YOU REALLY NEED TO RUN AND GET RAY?
I WAS THE ONE WHO GOT HIM. HE *NEARLY KILLED* THE GUYS WHO SOLD HER THOSE PILLS.
POLICE
*SIGH*... YOU IDIOT.
LOOK, DEREK, I *GOTTA* TAKE YOU IN NOW. I HAVE NO CHOICE. BETWEEN YOUR RECORD AND THOSE OTHER GUYS...
POLICE

...
WHAT IF THEY AIN'T HERE FOR A LITTLE WHILE?
WHAT ARE YOU TALKING ABOUT? SKIPPING TOWN?
NO... WELL, YES. BUT NOT REALLY.
POLICE
LOOK, I STILL GOT MY CAMP OUT IN THE BUSH. WHAT IF THEY STAY OUT THERE WITH ME FOR A LITTLE WHILE? JUST UNTIL THINGS CLEAR UP AROUND HERE?

FUCK THAT! I AM NOT GOING OUT INTO THE FUCKING BUSH! THIS IS RIDICULOUS!
OH, YOU GOT A BETTER IDEA? CAUSE IT'S EITHER THAT OR YOUR BROTHER THE FUCKING GENIUS HERE GOES AWAY FOR A WHILE AND YOU GO BACK DOWN TO TIMMINS.
BETH IS RIGHT. THIS *IS* CRAZY.
COME ON...THOSE BUGGERS UNDER THE BRIDGE HAVE HAD IT COMING FOR A WHILE, ALL THE SHIT THEY BRING UP HERE. WHO'S TO SAY THEY DIDN'T JUMP DEREK?
POLICE
I DON'T KNOW... I GUESS I COULD SELL IT. BUT YOU GUYS ARE REALLY PUTTING ME IN A SHITTY POSITION HERE.
LOOK, RAY, MAYBE THIS CAN WORK--
SHUT UP, DEREK.
POLICE

RAY, I'M SORRY, MAN. I KNOW I FUCKED UP. I KNOW YOU'RE TAKING A BIG RISK HERE.
DON'T BOTHER. I'VE HEARD IT ALL BEFORE. MAYBE YOU SHOULD *JUST* LEAVE.
POLICE
AT LEAST OUT IN THE BUSH YOU CAN'T FUCK ANYTHING ELSE UP.
...SO NOW WHAT?

WELL, HERE WE ARE...

WHAT A DUMP.

OH, I'M SORRY, PRINCESS. WHAT? YOU SPEND TOO MUCH TIME IN THE BIG CITY? FORGET YOU'RE A NORTHERN GIRL?
WHAT THE HELL YOU USE THIS FOR, AL?
STILL RUN A TRAPLINE OUT OF HERE. MARTEN. BEAVER.
DIDN'T YOUR MOM EVER TAKE YOU OUT TRAPPING WHEN YOU WERE A KID?
NAH, SHE NEVER REALLY TALKED ABOUT INDIAN STUFF.
INDIAN STUFF? HUMPH!

YOU OKAY?
NO. I FEEL LIKE SHIT. I CAN'T BELIEVE YOU DRAGGED ME OUT HERE. IT'S FUCKING FREEZING.
I'M SORRY, BETHY, BUT THIS IS GOING TO BE OKAY--
OH, FUCK OFF, DEREK! IT'S BAD ENOUGH YOU DRAGGED ME OUT HERE. JUST LEAVE ME THE FUCK ALONE.
BETHY--
COME ON, DEREK...

THIS WON'T BE AN EASY COUPLE OF DAYS.
GEE... YOU THINK?
YOU SURE YOU'RE GONNA BE OKAY ALONE WITH HER?
I'LL LIVE.
DRINK?
YOU SHOULDN'T HAVE THAT AROUND HER.
I AIN'T GONNA GIVE HER ANY. I'M NOT A RETARD, AL.
YOU SURE ABOUT THAT?

GONNA GO CHECK MY TRAPLINES WHILE I'M OUT HERE. THEN HEAD BACK. GOTTA WORK. YOU WANNA COME WITH? MIGHT LEARN SOMETHING.
I'LL PASS.
SUIT YOURSELF.
HERE. IT'S A SAT-PHONE. IN CASE YOU NEED SOMETHING. NO CELL TOWERS OUT HERE. I'LL BE BACK IN A COUPLE DAYS. I'LL BRING SOME MORE FOOD.
STAY WARM. KEEP THAT FIRE GOING.
AND, UH...YOU MIGHT WANNA TAKE THE KEY OUT OF THAT OTHER SNOW MACHINE.
...YEAH.

PANT-
PANT-PANT
PANT--PANT--

CRUNCH--CRUNCH--

HUSKY
RESTAURANT
OPEN 24 HOURS
CRUNCH--CRUNCH-CRUNCH

DING!
CAN I HELP YOU?
MAYBE...
BEEN LOOKING FOR MY GIRLFRIEND. SHE'S BEEN MISSING AND I'M REAL WORRIED.
YOU SEEN THIS GIRL IN THE LAST FEW DAYS?
...DON'T THINK SO.

DON'T THINK SO? YOU DON'T SOUND TOO SURE.
I'M SURE. HAVEN'T SEEN HER.
REALLY? CAUSE I'M REAL WORRIED ABOUT HER AND I'D HATE TO THINK OF *ANYTHING BAD* HAPPENING.
ESPECIALLY *ALL WAY UP HERE...* NOT TOO MANY PEOPLE AROUND TO HELP.
...

CRUNCH-CRUNCH--

11
PIMITAMON
120 Km

THOK

CRUNCH

HEY. GOT SOME MORE WOOD. I'LL WARM IT UP FOR YOU.
FUCKING FREEZING--
YOU STILL HAVE A FEVER.
DEREK, WAIT--

DEREK--
PLEASE...YOU GOTTA HELP ME. I CAN'T DO THIS.
I'M SORRY, BETHY... NO.
PLEASE, DEREK! THIS IS WHY I CAME BACK--SO YOU COULD HELP ME! PLEASE. YOU CAN GO AND GET ME SOME.
MAYBE IF I JUST CUT DOWN AT FIRST, WEAN MYSELF OFF...
...NO.

FUCK YOU!
YOU'RE JUST LIKE *HIM*, YOU KNOW THAT?!
YOU'RE A FUCKING DRUNK AND AN ASSHOLE!
--JUST LIKE HIM!

MORNING, TOUGH GUY.
AH!!

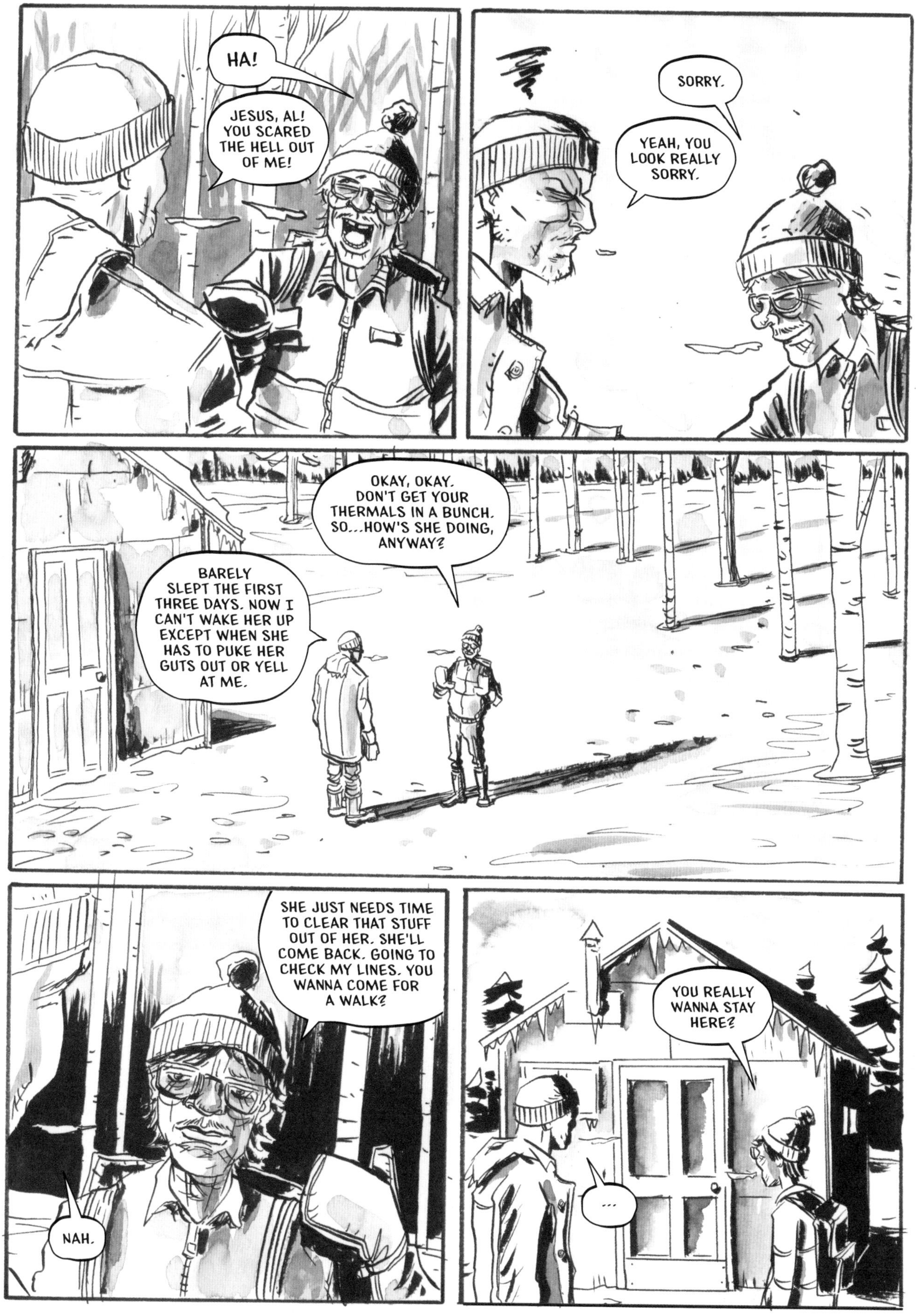
HA!
JESUS, AL! YOU SCARED THE HELL OUT OF ME!
SORRY.
YEAH, YOU LOOK REALLY SORRY.
OKAY, OKAY. DON'T GET YOUR THERMALS IN A BUNCH. SO...HOW'S SHE DOING, ANYWAY?
BARELY SLEPT THE FIRST THREE DAYS. NOW I CAN'T WAKE HER UP EXCEPT WHEN SHE HAS TO PUKE HER GUTS OUT OR YELL AT ME.
SHE JUST NEEDS TIME TO CLEAR THAT STUFF OUT OF HER. SHE'LL COME BACK. GOING TO CHECK MY LINES. YOU WANNA COME FOR A WALK?
NAH.
YOU REALLY WANNA STAY HERE?
...

CRUNCH. CRUNCH. CRUNCH.
SHHH!
WHAT?
MAYBE YOU COULD STOMP AROUND A BIT LOUDER? I DON'T THINK YOU'VE SCARED ALL THE ANIMALS AWAY QUITE YET.
WHAT THE HELL AM I SUPPOSED TO DO? FLY?
NO, BUT MAYBE TRY WALKING WITHOUT IT SOUNDING LIKE YOU GOT LEAD FEET.

COME ON, JUST A LITTLE BIT FURTHER.

UP HERE.
CRUNCH.
SO WHAT ARE YOU TRAPPING OUT HERE, ANYWAY?
FTTT!
MARTEN. THIS TRAP'S EMPTY, THOUGH.
HOW MUCH YOU GET FOR ONE?
MAYBE A HUNDRED, OR ONE-FIFTY FOR THE FUR. DEPENDS ON HOW COLD THE WINTER IS IN CHINA. THAT'S WHO'S BUYING FURS NOW.

WANT SOME TEA?
DON'T YOU GOT ANY COFFEE?
NO COFFEE. *REAL INDIANS* DRINK TEA IN THE BUSH.
BUT I'M ONLY HALF-INDIAN.
SO ONLY HAVE HALF A CUP.

CLOS

♫ MY LITTLE HORSIE, MY LITTLE HORSIE--I'LL BE RIGHT BY YOUR SIDE. ♩♩
MOMMY... CAN YOU HELP ME.
WHAT IS IT, SWEETIE? THE HAIR AGAIN?
YOU ALWAYS MANAGE TO GET THIS TANGLED, BETHY. JUST LIKE YOUR OWN HAIR.
MY HAIR *ISN'T* PINK, MOMMY.
NO. IT ISN'T.

DING
DADDY!
HOW ARE MY ANGELS TODAY?
GOOD. YOUR BEARD IS SCRATCHY.
HEH. SORRY.
AND HOW'S MY BEAUTIFUL WIFE?
COME ON, PAT...YOU KNOW JANUSZ DOESN'T LIKE YOU BEING IN HERE WHEN I'M CLOSING UP.
SCREW THAT OLD POLACK. YOU PRACTICALLY KEEP THIS PLACE RUNNING.

PAT...
FINE. LET'S GO, THEN.
I'M ALMOST DONE. I NEED TO FINISH CLEANING UP.
I SAID, *LET'S GO.* IT'S CLEAN ENOUGH.
I CAN'T *JUST LEAVE,* PAT. I NEED TO LOCK UP. JUST HOLD ON.
HERE, HAVE A *COFFEE.*
I DON'T WANT A DAMN COFFEE.
FINE. JUST *HOLD ON,* THEN.

DON'T TELL ME TO HOLD ON! I'VE BEEN LOCKED IN THAT FUCKING MILL ALL DAY. I WANT TO *GO HOME.*
...SMELLS LIKE YOU'VE BEEN IN THE BAR ALL DAY.
WHAT, I'M NOT ALLOWED TO STOP FOR A GODDAMN DRINK AFTER WORK ANYMORE?!
PAT!

YOU WANNA CLEAN THIS DUMP MORE'N COME HOME? FINE. CLEAN, THEN.
PAT!!

FUCKING BULLSHIT!
MOMMY?
IT'S OKAY, SWEETIE. DADDY JUST HAD A LONG DAY.
I'LL JUST CLEAN THIS UP AND WE'LL GO HOME, OKAY?
IT'S OKAY, MOMMY... I'LL HELP YOU.
--I'LL HELP YOU.

CRUNCH!

CRUNCH
CRUNCH-CRUNCH
CAN'T BELIEVE YOUR MOM NEVER TOOK YOU KIDS OUT MORE. SHE GREW UP IN WOODS LIKE THESE.
DIDN'T REALIZE YOU KNEW MOM SO WELL.
MARY? OH, I KNEW HER REAL GOOD, DEREK. REAL GOOD. WE PRACTICALLY GREW UP TOGETHER.

YOUR MOM WAS--WELL, SHE WAS A SWEET LADY. FUNNY TOO.
WE WENT TO THE SAME RESIDENTIAL SCHOOL IN FORT ALBANY. THEN WHEN WE WERE ABOUT YOUR AGE, A BUNCH OF US MOVED DOWN HERE TO THE PIT TO WORK IN THE MILL.
THEN SHE MET YOUR DAD AND--
WELL, I GUESS YOU KNOW ALL ABOUT HIM, EH?
...
HOW MANY MORE TRAPS WE GOTTA CHECK?
NOT MANY.
LET'S GO. GONNA BE DARK SOON.

O.P.P.
--HEY, RAY.
KNOCK!
WHAT'S UP, ANDY?
YOU KNOW THAT CALL YOU PUT IN TO DEAN TREMBLAY IN TIMMINS? WELL, HE PASSED IT ALONG, AND WE GOT A CALL FROM THE OPP IN COCHRANE...

A WAITRESS AT A HUSKY'S ALONG HIGHWAY 60 CALLED IN AN ALTERCATION WITH A GUY THAT FIT HIS DESCRIPTION.
GUY ALMOST BROKE THE OLD LADY'S WRIST.
074934671
LACHINE, WADE DANIEL
HEIGHT: 6'2"
WEIGHT: 206 lbs
EYES: GREEN
HAIR: BLONDE
TATTOO ON NECK
SEX: M
RACE: W
POSSESION
ASSAULT
ASSAULT
POSSESSION
18 months
3 years
18 months
probation
currently under investigation in relation to
RCMP case file #1229
THEY HAVEN'T SEEN HIM SINCE. THINK HE'S PROBABLY HEADED NORTH.
...SHIT.

CRUNCH - CRUNCH
CRUNCH - CRUNCH
BETH!!

WHAT THE HELL ARE YOU DOING OUT HERE?
NO KEY. COULDN'T LEAVE.
SHIT... HOLD ON.

DEREK...
WHAT?
I REALLY FUCKED UP.
JOIN THE CLUB.

NO. I MEAN-- DEREK...
I'M PREGNANT.
THAT'S WHY I LEFT WADE. WHEN HE FOUND OUT, HE--I HAD TO LEAVE.
JESUS, BETHY...
SAY SOMETHING, DEREK.

LET ME PUT SOME MORE WOOD ON. IT'S FREEZING IN HERE.
DEREK?
DO YOU-- DO YOU WANT TO KEEP IT? I MEAN--
I DON'T KNOW.
I DON'T KNOW WHAT I'M GONNA DO.
IT'S GONNA BE OKAY, BETHY.

EVERYTHING'S GONNA BE OKAY.

EEEEE

EEEEEE--
ZZZZZZ--
ZZZZ--SNRRT--
EEEEEE--
RAY.
MORNING.

EVERYTHING OKAY? YOU SEEM...
I'M FINE.
SHE FINALLY SLEPT THROUGH THE NIGHT. THAT'S SOMETHING.
HOW ARE THINGS IN TOWN? AM I OFF THE MOST WANTED LIST YET?
...
POLICE
RAY?
THINGS ARE OKAY. PROBABLY BEST IF YOU STAY OUT HERE FOR A BIT LONGER, THOUGH.
WELL, YOU CAN BRING ME SOME *MORE RATIONS* IF YOU'RE FEELING GENEROUS. RUNNING LOW.
I DON'T THINK SO.
ARE YOU SERIOUS?

I DON'T THINK THAT'S A VERY GOOD IDEA, DEREK.
POLICE
DON'T WORRY, I'LL KEEP IT AWAY FROM BETH.
IT'S NOT BETH I'M WORRIED ABOUT.
FUCK YOU, RAY! I DON'T NEED YOUR HOLIER-THAN-THOU SHIT. NOT NOW!
WHERE YOU GOING?
CRUNCH
WHAT THE FUCK IS IT TO YOU? WHY DON'T YOU FUCK OFF BACK TO TOWN, SHERIFF.
CRUNCH - CRUNCH - CRUNCH

CRUNCH...
CRUNCH-
-CRUNCH
PANT-- PANT- PANT-.

ARK!
ARK!

HEY!
CRUNCH...
CRUNCH.

--RANGERS ARE DOWN BY TWO LATE IN THE SECOND PERIOD.
--PANT--PANT--PANT--

--AND MINNESOTA CLEARLY HAS THE MOMENTUM NOW.
THEY'LL HAVE TO MAKE ONE LAST PUSH HERE IF THEY WANT TO TIE THIS ONE UP...

RANGERS TRY TO BREAK OUT OF THEIR ZONE AS RICHARDS DISHES OFF TO OUELETTE.
SKRUNCH!

OH, AND HAGLUND TAKES A RUN AT BIG OUELETTE.
I CAN'T BELIEVE OUELETTE IS GETTING UP FROM THAT ONE. THEY DON'T MAKE THEM MUCH TOUGHER THAN THIS GUY, THOUGH...

AND OUELETTE DOESN'T LIKE THAT HIT AT ALL!

OH MY!
I MEAN--I KNOW THAT HAGLUND HIT OUELETTE FIRST BUT THAT WAS JUST--
--MY GOD, THAT WAS A VICIOUS ATTACK!
--AND OUELETTE WILL BE SUSPENDED FOR THAT--
HE'LL BE LUCKY IF HE EVER PLAYS AGAIN!

ARK!

ARK!
STOP!
CRUNCH.. CRUNCH..

PANT-- PANT-- PANT-
WELL, IF IT ISN'T BIGFOOT. HEARD YOU STOMPING AROUND ABOUT TEN MINUTES AGO. FIGURED IT WAS EITHER YOU OR AN ELEPHANT GOT LOOSE IN THE BUSH.
YOU OKAY? LOOK LIKE YOU SEEN A GHOST.

NO... I--IT'S NOTHING.
WELL, THEN, COME HERE AND SEE THIS.
WHAT?
YOU BAITED THIS TRAP YESTERDAY, REMEMBER?
I DID?
YEP. THIS IS YOUR FIRST MARTEN.
SHIT.
THERE YOU GO, TOUGH GUY. YOU CAN MAKE YOURSELF A HAT.
SECOND THOUGHT, YOU MIGHT NEED TWO MARTENS TO COVER THEM BIG EARS OF YOURS.

CRUNCH... CRUNCH
BETH?
WHAT'S WRONG?
I'M OKAY. JUST WARMER DOWN HERE.

WELL, THE FIRE'S LOW. HOW YOU FEELING OTHERWISE?
LIKE I'M A TOTAL MESS.
YEAH? WELL, SO AM I. WHERE DOES THAT LEAVE US?
FREEZING OUR ASSES OFF IN THE BUSH TOGETHER.
YEAH. PRETTY MUCH.

HOW LONG YOU BEEN TAKING THAT STUFF?
MAYBE A FEW YEARS. I DON'T KNOW.
DID THIS GUY, WADE. DID HE START YOU ON IT?
NO. STARTED BEFORE HIM.
MY FRIENDS AND I USED TO JUST DRINK A LOT AFTER WORK. ONE NIGHT SOMEONE HAD SOME OF THESE BLUE PILLS WITH HER... SHE CRUSHED THEM UP AND WE SNORTED THEM. IT BLEW EVERYTHING AWAY. BOOZE...EVERYTHING.
STARTED TAKING THEM BEFORE MY SHIFT. I COULD HAVE THE SHITTIEST DAY EVER AND IT DIDN'T MATTER. I FELT GREAT.
LOST MY JOB. GOT A JOB AT A SHITTIER BAR. WADE AND HIS FRIENDS USED TO COME IN THERE... HE ALWAYS HAD STUFF ON HIM.

SO...YOU SEEN *HIM* LATELY... DAD?
FUCK NO.
LAST I HEARD HE WAS DOWN IN COCHRANE SOMEWHERE WORKING AT THE MILL DOWN THERE.
WHY DO YOU THINK MOM MARRIED A GUY LIKE HIM?
WHAT? A WHITE GUY?
NO... A DRUNK ASSHOLE.
I DON'T KNOW. WHY WERE YOU WITH WADE?

...SORRY.
IT'S OKAY.
YOU KNOW AL AND MOM CAME FROM THE SAME RES. WORKED AT THE MILL IN THE PIT TOGETHER...BEFORE DAD. BEFORE THE ACCIDENT.
YOU EVER THINK ABOUT IT? THE ACCIDENT, I MEAN? YOU WERE PRETTY LITTLE. DO YOU REALLY REMEMBER IT?
I DON'T KNOW. I THINK SO...

"I WAS IN THE BACKSEAT.
"I JUST REMEMBER HANGING THERE UPSIDE DOWN...
"I WASN'T SCARED. I JUST DIDN'T UNDERSTAND WHAT WAS GOING ON.
"I REMEMBER YOU SAYING...
...IT'S OKAY, BETHY. DON'T LOOK. DON'T LOOK AT MOM.

"THEN I REMEMBER WAITING. WAITING WITH YOU UNTIL THE COPS CAME.
"...AND THEN SHE WAS JUST GONE."

YOU THINK I CAN DO IT DEREK?
WHAT? KICK THAT STUFF? YEAH. I DO.
NO, NOT JUST THAT. I MEAN, DO YOU REALLY THINK I COULD BE A MOM?
...YEAH. I DO.

I'M BEAT. WANT TO GO TO SLEEP?
I DON'T THINK I CAN GET BACK UP ON THE BED.
...SO DON'T.
YOU'RE RIGHT. IT IS WARMER DOWN HERE.

SKY RANCH DINER
BUD LITE
The PIT STOP
The PIT STOP

CAN I HELP YOU?
LOOKING FOR DEREK OUELETTE, OR HIS SISTER. OLD FRIENDS OF MINE. YOU SEEN THEM?

RRRRRRRRRRRRRRRRRRRRRRRRRRR

CRUNCH..
RRRRRRRR--
YOU FINALLY COME TO PUT US OUT OF OUR MISERY, AL?

YOU AIN'T THAT LUCKY. WE'RE GOING HUNTING.
BIT MUCH FOR MARTEN, ISN'T IT?
BEEN TRACKING A MOOSE ABOUT FIVE MILES DOWN RIVER. BIG ONE.
NICE TO SEE YOU OUT OF YOUR COCOON, MISSY. WANNA COME WITH US? GETS BORING OUT THERE JUST THE TWO OF US.
NAH...I DON'T LIKE GUNS.

FAIR ENOUGH. KEEP THAT STOVE GOING...WE'RE GONNA EAT WELL TONIGHT!
YOU SURE YOU'RE OKAY HERE?
YEAH. I'M SURE.
OKAY. SEE YOU LATER.
SEE YOU.

BETHY-- WAKE UP!
WE HAVE TO WAKE UP, BETHY...WE HAVE TO GO.
YAWN
WHERE ARE WE GOING, MOMMY? I'M TIRED.
I KNOW. JUST ON A LITTLE TRIP, SWEETIE.

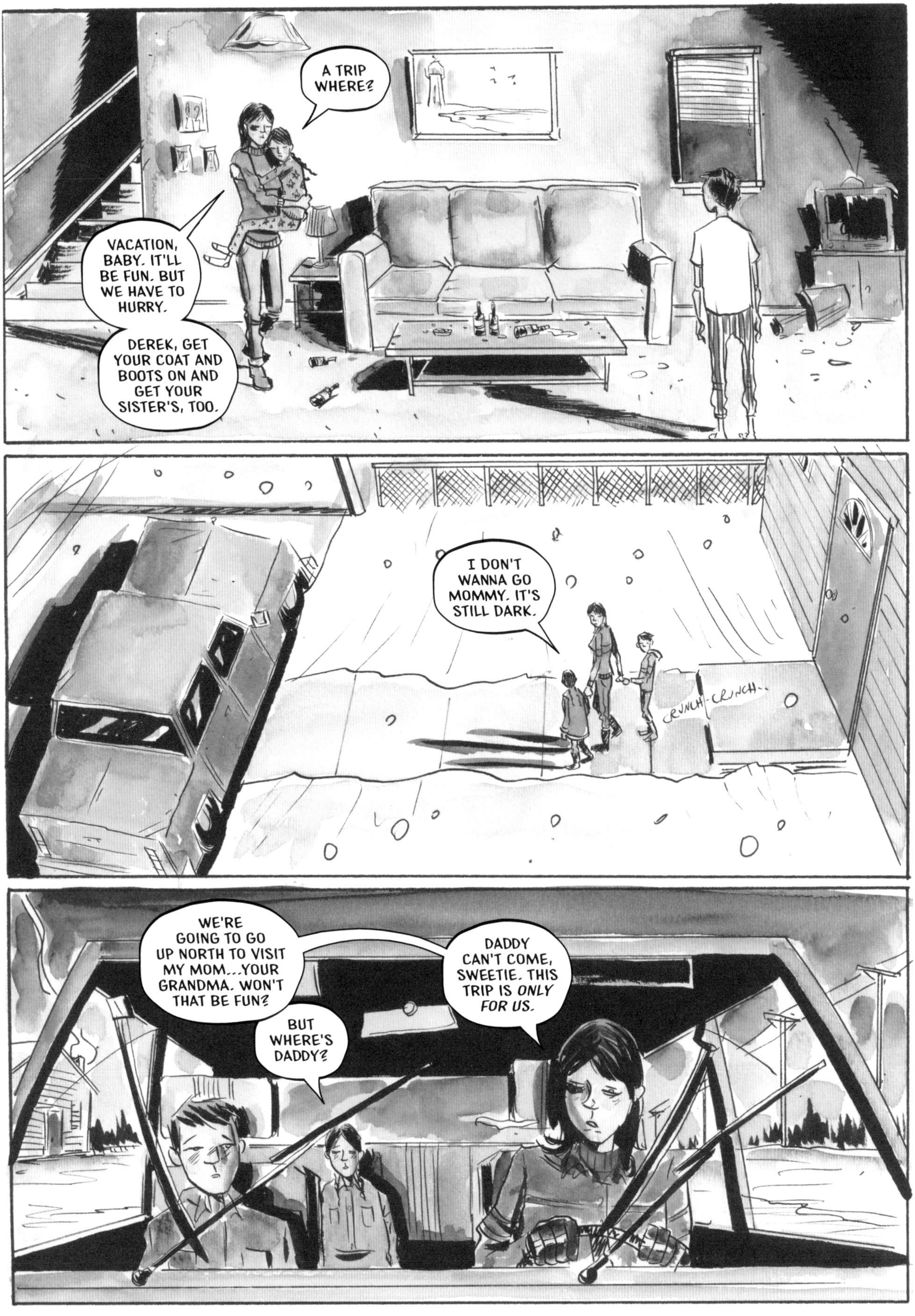
A TRIP WHERE?
VACATION, BABY. IT'LL BE FUN. BUT WE HAVE TO HURRY.
DEREK, GET YOUR COAT AND BOOTS ON AND GET YOUR SISTER'S, TOO.
I DON'T WANNA GO MOMMY. IT'S STILL DARK.
CRUNCH-CRUNCH
WE'RE GOING TO GO UP NORTH TO VISIT MY MOM...YOUR GRANDMA. WON'T THAT BE FUN?
BUT WHERE'S DADDY?
DADDY CAN'T COME, SWEETIE. THIS TRIP IS *ONLY* FOR US.

IT'S GOING TO BE OKAY, SWEETIE.
THINGS WILL BE BETTER, I PROMISE.
WE DON'T NEED HIM ANYMORE.
CRUNCH
CRUNCH

SCREEECH...

BETHY?
IT'S OKAY, MOM. I'M HERE.

BEEP! BEEP
--KT--
HELLO?
RAY?
BETH? WHAT'S WRONG? DID SOMETHING HAPPEN?!
RAY, I NEED YOU TO COME PICK ME UP. THERE'S SOMETHING I GOTTA DO.

PIMITAMON

CRUNCH

Pimitamon
ARENA
POLICE

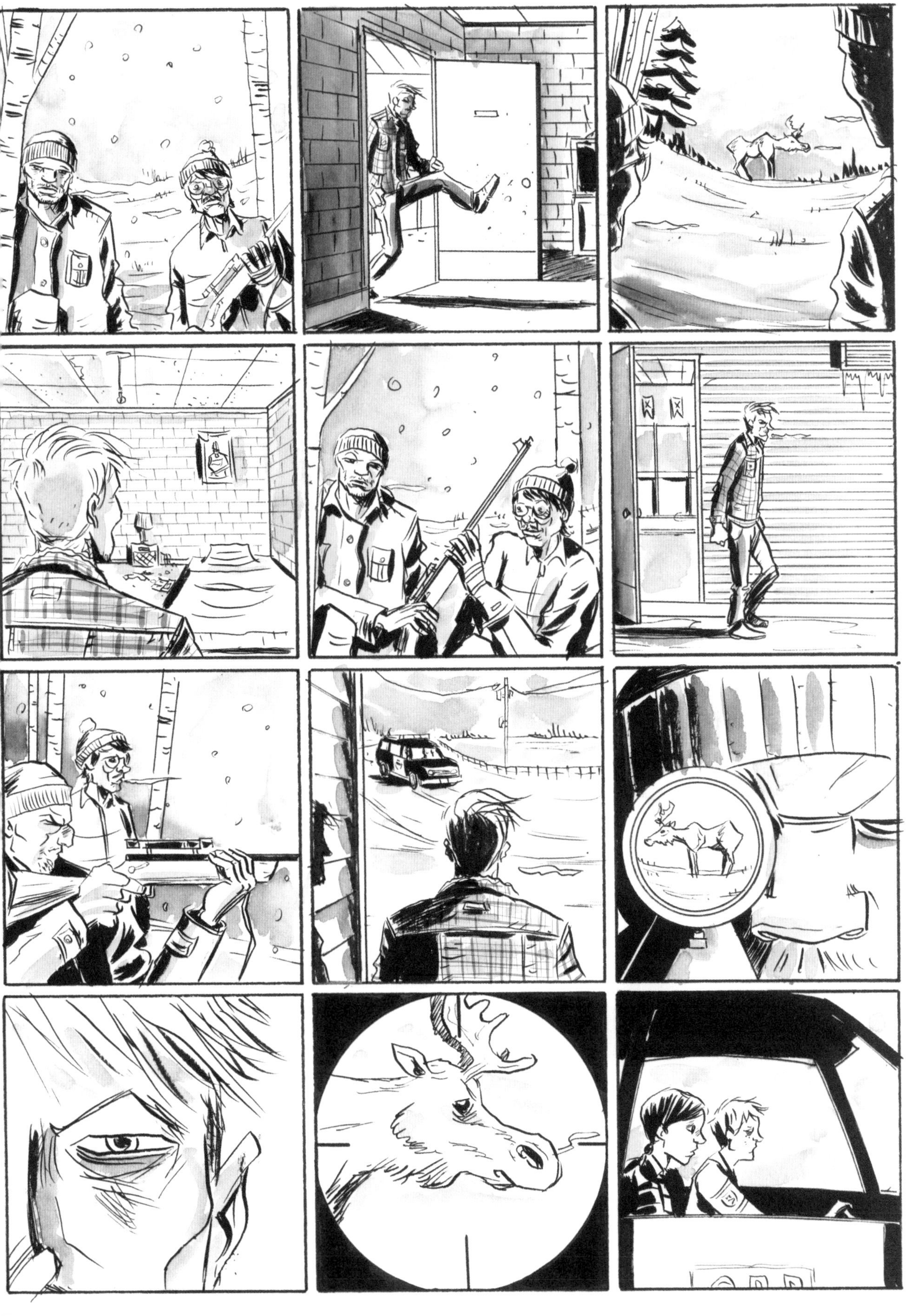

BLAM!

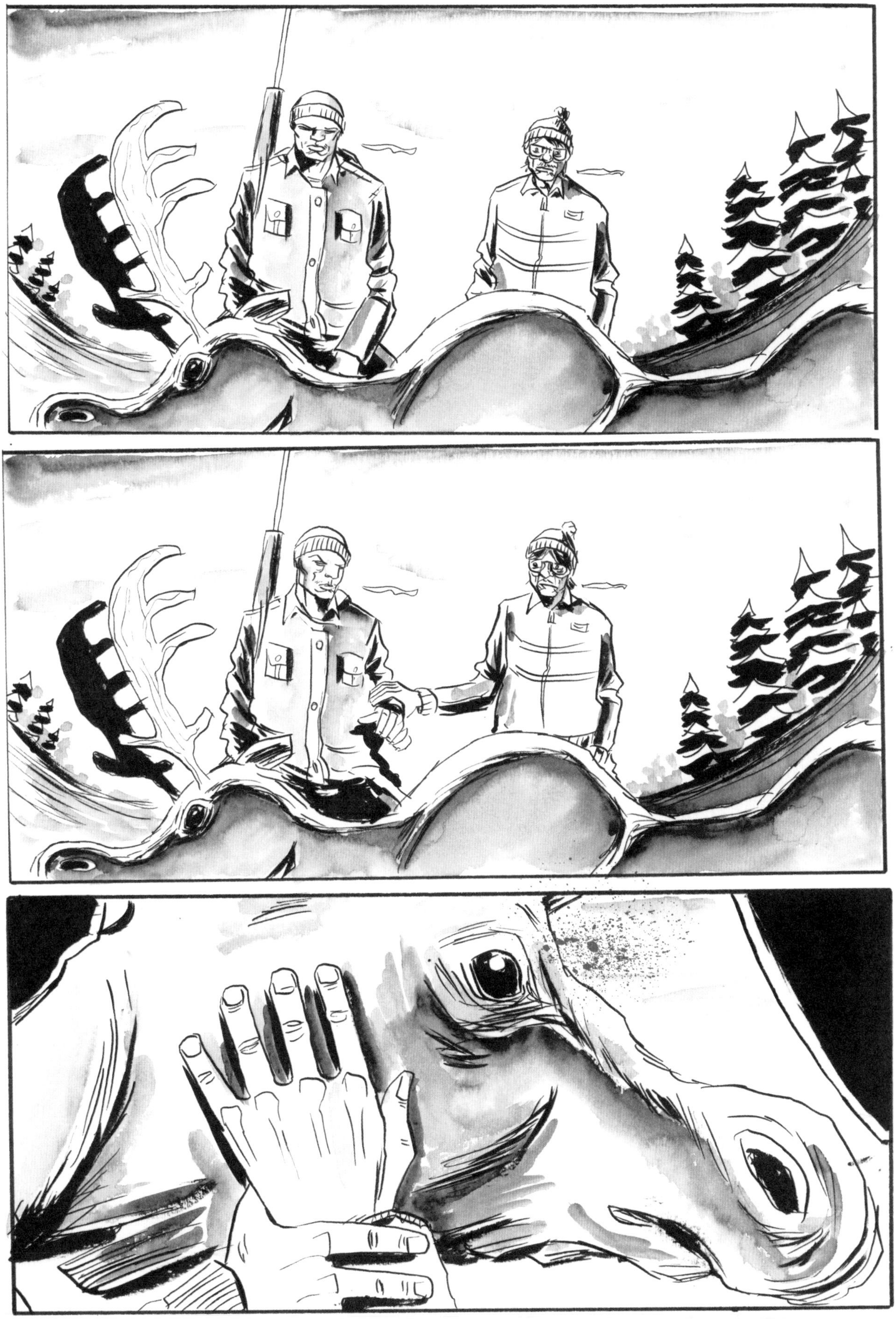

TIMBERC. CO.
POLICE
O.P.P.
YOU SURE YOU DON'T WANT ME TO COME WITH YOU?
I'M SURE. THANKS FOR THIS, RAY...FOR EVERYTHING. YOU'VE ALWAYS KIND OF LOOKED OUT FOR DEREK AND ME SINCE WE WERE KIDS, AND--
S'OKAY. I--I MISSED HAVING YOU AROUND, BETH.

CAN I HELP YOU, SWEETHEART?
DAD... IT'S ME.

Cola
SAFETY STARTS WITH YOU
SMOKE?
Dunavin Light
NO.
SO...DIDN'T EXPECT TO SEE YOU. I HOPE YOU AIN'T COME FOR ANY MONEY. I AIN'T GOT NONE.

I DON'T WANT MONEY.
OKAY. SO... WHAT DO YOU WANT?
I GUESS I JUST WANTED TO SEE YOU.
HEH... WELL, HERE I AM.
DAMN, YOU SURE GREW UP PRETTY, GIRL. YOU LOOK JUST LIKE YOUR MOM, YOU KNOW THAT.
*DON'T.* DON'T YOU TALK ABOUT HER.
OH, WHAT'S THIS? YOU COME TO BLAME ME FOR ALL YOUR BULLSHIT? WELL, BOO-HOO. WE ALL GOT SHIT TO DEAL WITH, KID.
'SIDES, THAT BROTHER OF YOURS SEEMED TO MAKE OUT OKAY. PLAYING HOCKEY.
PROBABLY RICH. BUT I DON'T SEE NONE OF THAT MONEY, DO I?
HE'S NOT RICH. HE'S A MESS, JUST LIKE ME. BUT I'M NOT HERE TO BLAME YOU.

SEE, I KNOW MEN LIKE YOU. I'VE *BEEN WITH MEN LIKE YOU.* AND I KNOW WHY YOU ARE THE WAY YOU ARE.
YOU'RE SCARED.
FUCK YOU. I AIN'T SCARED OF SHIT.
YES... YOU ARE.
YOU'RE SCARED OF EVERYTHING. SCARED OF DYING. SCARED OF BEING WEAK. SO YOU GOTTA HIT AND HURT EVERYTHING AROUND YOU TO PROVE HOW TOUGH YOU ARE.

YOU WANNA HIT ME? HUH? THAT MAKE YOU FEEL BETTER? GO AHEAD.
NO. I JUST WANTED YOU TO SEE THAT *I'M STILL HERE.* YOU--YOU ALMOST KILLED ME. BUT I'M STILL HERE.
AND I CAME TO TELL YOU THAT SHE WASN'T SCARED ANYMORE EITHER. SHE WAS LEAVING YOU.
WHAT?
MOM. SHE DIDN'T *NEED* YOU ANYMORE.
THE NIGHT SHE DIED. SHE WAS *LEAVING YOU.* SHE WAS FINALLY TAKING US AND GOING.

BUT THE ACCIDENT--SHE NEVER GOT A CHANCE TO GET AWAY FROM YOU. AND YOU KNOW WHAT...I REALIZED I NEVER GOT AWAY EITHER.
BUT NOW I AM.
WE ARE.
I'VE MADE A LOT OF MISTAKES... A LOT OF BAD DECISIONS. BUT... WELL, I'M GOING TO HAVE A BABY, DAD.
I DIDN'T THINK I WAS GOING TO TELL YOU THAT, BUT MAYBE THAT'S WHY I REALLY CAME. I WANTED YOU TO KNOW.
I WANTED YOU TO KNOW THAT I'M GOING TO HAVE A BABY AND YOU'LL *NEVER KNOW* YOUR OWN GRANDCHILD. NEVER MEET HIM. NEVER SEE HIM. NEVER TOUCH HIM.

HE'LL NEVER KNOW YOU **EVER EXISTED.**
Cola
WE DON'T NEED YOU ANYMORE EITHER.

SEE, I TOLD YOU NOT TO WORRY. SHE'S WITH RAY.

OPP
YOU OKAY? I WAS WORRIED SICK!
I'M FINE. REALLY.
WE JUST HAD TO RUN AN ERRAND.
POLICE
THAT IS VILE.
AW, COME ON...DON'T TELL ME YOU WENT VEGETARIAN IN THE BIG CITY, BETHY? WE'RE HAVING FRESH MOOSE STEW!
...THAT DOES SMELL REALLY GOOD ACTUALLY.

CRUNCH
POLICE

SO, AL... DEREK SAID YOU KNEW MUM?
OH, YEAH. WE GREW UP TOGETHER IN FORT ALBANY.
YOU EVER GO BACK UP THERE?
YEAH. TRY TO GO EVERY YEAR. STILL GOT FAMILY UP THERE.
SO DO YOU, YOU KNOW...YOUR GOHKUM IS STILL THERE. AND YOU GOT LOTS OF UNCLES. COUSINS.
MAN, I'M FULL. NEED A SMOKE.

YOU GUYS EVER WANT TO GO UP THERE SOMETIME, JUST LET ME KNOW.
CRUNCH-CRUNCH..
THAT MIGHT BE COOL.

--KRRST--
RAY, YOU
THERE?
HEY, RAY,
THINK ANDY'S
CALLING
YOU...
AH,
SHIT.
UH-OH, KOJAK.
TROUBLE IN THE
PIT. MAYBE DR. DON
IS SELLING HIS
"OVERSTOCK" IN
THE BACK ALLEY
AGAIN.
POLICE
RAY, COME
IN. WE GOT
TROUBLE. THAT
GUY YOU TOLD ME
TO LOOK OUT
FOR--
--WADE
LACHINE--I
JUST SEEN HIM
ON MAIN
STREET.

DID YOU KNOW ABOUT THIS, RAY?!
I--I DIDN'T KNOW HE WAS HERE, BUT--
WELL, WHAT THE FUCK ARE YOU GOING TO DO ABOUT IT?!
POLICE
YOU NEED TO LET ME HANDLE THIS, DEREK. THE RCMP ARE WATCHING THIS GUY, TOO. THEY WANT HIM FOR SOME BIG DRUG CASE. FOR NOW WE JUST GOTTA HOLD OFF AND--
OH, FUCK THAT!
LISTEN TO ME. THIS IS COMPLICATED... UNLESS HE ACTUALLY BREAKS THE LAW, DOES SOMETHING, I CAN'T TOUCH HIM, DEREK!
DEREK, PLEASE. YOU DON'T KNOW WADE. HE'S MIXED UP IN SOME BAD SHIT. IF RAY SAYS--
WHY DO YOU THINK HE'S HERE, BETHY? FOR YOU. THIS GUY AIN'T JUST GOING TO LEAVE.

THAT'S EXACTLY WHY I NEED YOU TO STAY HERE!
NO. NO WAY.
POLICE
POL
YOU NEED TO CALM DOWN, DEREK. LISTEN TO RAY--
FUCK THAT! YOU AIN'T GOING TO DO SOMETHING ABOUT THIS GUY, *I WILL!*
O.P.P
DEREK, STOP! JUST STOP!
GET YOUR HANDS OFF OF ME, RAY!
OPP

I SAID, GET OFF!
DEREK!
POLICE
U.P.D

STOP!

DEREK, DON'T DO THIS!
PLEASE.
...
DEREK!!!

HE TOOK MY SNOW MACHINE, BUT I'LL TAKE THE OTHER ONE AND CATCH UP TO HIM, DON'T WORRY.
NO, HE HAS THE KEY!
RAY, HE'LL KILL HIM!
JUST CALM DOWN. I WON'T LET THAT HAPPEN.
LET'S GO, THEN!
WHAT ARE YOU DOING!?
EITHER YOU START THE DAMNED TRUCK OR I WALK TO TOWN AND FREEZE ON THE WAY. YOUR CHOICE, RAY!
DON'T LOOK AT ME. SHE'S AS PIGHEADED AS HER DAMN BROTHER.

PIMITAMON

DEREK! AIN'T SEEN YOU IN A LONG TIME, MAN.
YEAH... BEEN BUSY.
LISTEN, I'M LOOKING FOR SOMEONE...
--SHIT, YEAH. YOUR OLD HOCKEY BUDDY, RIGHT?
HOCKEY BUDDY?
EXIT
YEAH, MAN. BIG GUY LIKE YOU. HE'S BEEN COMING IN HERE LAST TWO NIGHTS. ASKING FOR YOU.

YOU KNOW WHERE HE'S STAYING?
YEAH, I THINK HE'S UP AT THE POLAR BEAR.
SIT DOWN, MAN! GAME'S ON. AND HEY, SORRY ABOUT THE OTHER WEEK WHEN I WOULDN'T SERVE YOU, MAN...YOU KNOW HOW IT IS. HERE, HAVE A SHOT ON ME.
DEREK?
BUD
I'M GOOD.

ARK! ARK!
WELL... COME ON, THEN.
ARK!
CRUNCH.
CRUNCH.

HURRY UP, RAY!
I AM!
POLICE
DEREK IS GOING TO KILL HIM, RAY...
CRUNCH
CRUNCH
CRUNCH
--HE'LL KILL HIM!

POLAR BEAR LODGE
ARK!

SNNNRRRRRT..
--THE FUCK?
ARK!
ARK! ARK!
WILL YOU SHUT THE FUCK--

WELL, WELL...DIDN'T EXPECT IT WOULD BE THIS EASY TO FIND YOU.
WHERE IS SHE?

AIN'T SMART YOU COMING HERE.
YOU DEAF OR JUST STUPID? WHERE THE FUCK IS BETH?
WHAP

THE FUCK IS WRONG WITH YOU?! HUH? I WILL FUCK YOU UP!
THINK I'M SCARED OF YOU, DEREK? YOU ARE *WRONG.*
WHERE IS SHE?!

ANSWER ME YOU DUMB FUCK!

JUNKIE BITCH IS PREGNANT, YOU KNOW THAT? SHE TELL YOU THAT?
THAT'S MY GODDAMN KID!
THE FUCK IS WRONG WITH YOU!? FUCKING FIGHT BACK YOU PIECE OF SHIT!

FIGHT--
--BACK!

THUD!

GET UP! GET UP!

AW, WHAT THE FUCK IS--
DEREK!
PUT YOUR HANDS BEHIND YOUR HEAD!!
THIS IS BULLSHIT!

BETH?!
BETH-- THIS IS BULLSHIT!
DEREK-- WHAT DID YOU DO?
I LET IT GO, BETHY.

DEREK?

POLICE